# LIBERATION OF RRIBAN

## Christopher Blythe Bartram

Christopher Blythe Bartram / ISBN-13: 9780692581230

## DEDICATION

To Rose, your absence is strongly felt today as it was yesterday.

# CONTENTS

Acknowledgments    I

PART 1

1    Introduction        3

2                        Pg 4.2

3                        Pg 8

4                        Pg 14.2

4.2                      Pg 19

6                        Pg 23

7                        Pg 31

8                        Pg 37


PART 2

9                        Pg 57

10                       Pg 64

11                       Pg 74

12                       Pg 82

13                       Pg 87

14                       Pg 96

14.2                     Pg 111

16                       Pg 121

17                       Pg 128

Christopher Blythe Bartram / ISBN-13: 9780692581230

18                              Pg 134

            One Month Later     Pg 149

            The End             Pg 150

            Author's notes      Pg 152

Christopher Blythe Bartram / ISBN-13: 9780692581230

# ACKNOWLEDGMENTS

Jeffrey Chang / The Designer

Madeline E. Buhr / The Editor

Christopher Blythe Bartram / ISBN-13: 9780692581230

# CHAPTER 1
# INTRODUCTION

Welcome to the third book in the Dark Knight Series. The first book attempted to put into question what we believe to be good or bad. The second book took the first question further by asking if good or bad was just a matter of perception. One country's freedom fighter is another country's terrorist after all.

The Republic with their White Knight protectors originated from Earth just like the Dark Empire and their Dark Knight guardians. The Republic and the White Knights originally were the countries of North Korea, Russia, and elements of various groups in the Middle East. North Korea took a commanding role in this alliance to form what is now known as the Republic. For the longest time, they had kept their country isolated from the rest of the world. Their leaders controlled everything from what you ate to what you saw to what you believed in and why. In the end, they even controlled how you felt.

All countries on Earth were equally guilty in this. What set North Korea aside was the level to which this was done to their own people. The groups in the Middle East were quick to hate America and its allies because their people lived in a different way than how Middle Easterners believed they should live. Taking the lands and cities by force again, and by controlling the minds of the people, they conquered by forcefully determining what and how the people felt.

It was only a matter of time. Every year it seemed to get close to all-out war. They kept coming to the edge of the world imploding before North Korea backed down, like a lion in a zoo rearing its head with nowhere to go. To the rest of the world, North Korea was a repressed country with a ruthless dictator, guilty of unspeakable acts. This was the same for two separate countries, who were to become part of the NATO and United Nation groups, Japan and Germany, and let us not forget Italy. During the twentieth century, there was a conflict between the Allied forces and the Axis alliance. The exact same things the people of America were influenced to believe about Germany are the same things people were led to believe about North Korea.

It worked, for one, because not too many people ever picked up a history book or watched the documentaries. When it began happening in front of them, they didn't see the same magic acts being performed. The one time the propaganda machine might have failed for the NATO forces, depending on your view, was when they were caught in a lie. They led a campaign to get everyone behind a military conflict based on the hypothesis there was "weapons of mass destruction," as they were considered back then. When their forces went in and never found anything, it put them all in a difficult position, described as being caught with your pants down. However, with the theme that the governments only let their people believe what they wanted them to believe, it is more than likely. They did find these weapons however, and whatever they found they decided to keep secret from the world. It is said "ignorance is bliss," and it could very well be just that. They could have decided the world staying ignorant would be far better than knowing what they actually found.

Once the information was out, after the files had been declassified, if they had known what was eventually realized it may not have been possible for people to go about their lives without looking over their shoulders. As a result, their leaders decided to be seen as liars rather than admit the truth and take away the world's innocence. We all remember how we felt when we found out the tooth fairy was just our parents.

This reinforces everything said from before, what you believe to be right or wrong. The concepts of good and bad have been taught over time and put into our minds. And so we must question, who is controlling your mind?

Have you ever wondered why you suddenly feel hungry while watching the ads and previews before a movie starts in a theater? Ever wondered why you don't like a certain place or country even though you've never been there? Have you ever wondered why you may feel aggressive when you see the color orange?

Do you make your choices or is the media influencing your choices for you?

I ask you again; who is controlling your mind?

# CHAPTER 2

There was almost silence, just the low hum of machines and creaking of the metal plates of the ship expanding and contracting as the ship's atmosphere was adjusted using the controls to suit the crew's needs, neither too hot nor too cold. The shift on duty covered the bridge, keeping watch as the remainder of the crew had been ordered to get some rest. There were three look outs on duty: one looking forward, one looking to the right and one to the left. For the areas they couldn't see, there were two extra men on duty watching the display panels of the sensors. This was the night watch of the Dragomire Dreadnaught of the Dark Empire, accompanied by the Morgan Rice, which was guarding a small flotilla of smaller crafts with a couple of escort ships. The look out to the right used his glasses to look at the Morgan Rice and saw the name displayed proudly under a spotlight.

As funny as the term sounded, being this was space and it was always dark like night, this was the small crew that guarded the ship during night time, times when there was no activity and the majority of the crew was asleep. That was the standing order for nighttime, to get as much sleep as possible. The officer who picked the short straw to work this watch was fast asleep in his chair. A young dark ensign, the crew liked him enough and did not mind too much that he was younger than most of them, but they were still reluctant to salute him as an officer. The second lookout looking ahead took a deep breath in and blew out to steam up the window with his breath. The he started to play tic-tac-toe with himself. He lost.

"How is that even possible?" he said. He was in his early thirties, stood six feet tall with a short beard and shaved head, and was dressed in his traditional dark military uniform.

"You were always too smart for your own good; you out smarted even yourself." The look out to the left laughed with the last look out. They were twin boys, now in their mid-twenties, native to Rriban. Having grown up on the planet, they were in their teens at the time of the attack.

"What are we even doing out here? We been here for days and told to sit and wait; wait for what is what I like to know. We are sitting targets, you mark my words. We will be targeted and destroyed. This is a mistake," said Cole, the lookout to the right.

"I've told you before, no one is looking for us. No one even knows we are here; no one will be out to kill us. If anyone comes here, it will be purely accidental," his brother, Cody, said.

"That doesn't make sense either," remarked the lookout looking forward.

"Go on then, explain why, Waller." Cody turned, waving his hand as if to usher him forward before returning to look out the window.

"We have been positioned here with a small fleet. We are clearly waiting for something or someone, so logically someone must know we are here. Why else would we be here just sitting for as long as we have? The Admiral is excited, so you know whatever it is, it has to be big. I can't imagine anything getting the old man excited being as old as he is. There can't be that many things that excites him anymore," Waller finished saying, just as he finished another game of tic-tac-toe. This time he tied with himself.

"Well I hope whatever it is, it happens soon," Cole stated.

"What's the rush? Not like you have anyone waiting for you. That piece of skirt will be in bed with the next pair of warm legs she come across." A bored Cody was attempting to provoke his brother.

"That isn't true. She said she would quit being a waitress at the tavern when I come back. She wants to be with me," Cole replied with a hurt voice.

"Did you not learn yet? Never fall in love with a bar waitress. They want you to buy drinks and a depressed customer is only beaten by a love sick fool, and then there will be a depressed love sick fool when your hopes are crushed. You are walking…well, sleeping into her plan. She wants money, and for you to keep buying drinks at the tavern," Waller said with a sad expression of pity on his face.

"That is enough of the chatter men; stay focused. Scopes?" The voice of the ensign, who they all thought was asleep, suddenly came from nowhere. He was nineteen, but had the face of a baby, which led to his nickname "Baby face". Despite his age, he had not been able to grow any hair or stubble on his chin.

"What is the score, Waller? ...and Cody leave your brother alone. Cole, if that is what she told you, then I wish for your sake it is true and you are happy together. Just don't start planning anything until you see her last pay stub." He apparently didn't miss anything while he was seemingly asleep.

"Starboard clear!" Cole shouted,

"Bow clear!" Waller remarked "1 loss, 2 ties and 4 wins, Sir."

"Port clear," Cody echoed.

"Scanners clea—" one of the other crewmen watching the scanners was about to report. "Hey Bellis, do you see that sector A9?"

The man looked up towards his partner.

"I did once, not anymore." Bellis looked over and saw the blip appear once again on his partners screen "Sir, not sure, possible spook. I saw it on my screen, then it went. I would say weapons fire far off," reported Bellis.

"Sir!" the original crew member watching the scanner, Jason, shouted. "Far off, picking up a transponder signal of the Dark Intelligence. They are still a long way, far away, but won't be for long," he finished reporting.

The Dark Ensign Bollinger got up and walked over to the screen.

"You are lucky, Waller; you clearly are distracted tonight." As he looked down, he confirmed what was reported to him.

"Sir," Cody started to say, "Should we not tell the old man?"

"Don't worry, this will tell him." As the ensign leaned over, he pressed a red circular button, sounding the alarm all throughout the ship.

# CHAPTER 3

"The situation is this simple. They have created a bottle neck at the point of entrance at the district, with a firing range of a quarter mile long. In between is a no man's land; anyone caught in that gap is shot down by either side. We have formed up most of the army here at the former intelligence building." The voice of Rockwell continued, "I have placed sharp shooters on the roofs of buildings, with spotters to watch and make sure they don't try to come in or out from anywhere else. We have them surrounded. We have been forced to stop sending the fighters in. They have in their possession a working gun battery, which was reported to have been disabled by my initial landing force. Clearly they were wrong, as the evidence is laying in pieces scattered across the non-republic district."

"How many forces do we have now?" asked Commander Jere. He had been promoted to replace the late commander Eddington after his assassination.

"We have total number of forty four thousand with all the forces pulled in from all major points of the planet, together with cooks, supply clerks and anyone that can hold a gun. Master Sergio reported in and intercepted a ship leaving orbit and is in pursuit. They will return and re-supply us with what they have free," Rockwell replied.

"Waller and I have no problem getting the people out of no man's land. There still some of our people that are laying out there wounded. The problem is if we try to go close, we get fired at," Chester explained. A sturdy man, he was one of the commanders in the remote cities, in charge of the garrison. His rank was really the same as Rockwell. However, there can only be one leader and since Rockwell was senior to Chester, Chester was referred to as Commander.

"The simple truth of what needs to be done is straight forward. You need to offer a ceasefire, allow both sides to retrieve their wounded," said Ramon, the leader of the White Knight garrison on Rriban.

"If I give them a ceasefire I will be validating their position, appearing to accept them as a military force when they are nothing but a bunch of angry civilian,." retorted Rockwell.

"These 'bunch of angry civilians' captured and secured two armored units, killed four White Knights, including masters, shot down fighters, subverted your own personal cooks and your own office clerk. Not bad for an angry mob." Commander Powell spoke up, clearly putting in his opinion. He was growing tired of his general's attitude.

The other commanders in the room all murmured their consent. It was Douglas next who spoke with an idea.

"Sir, you have no choice; offer the ceasefire. The worse that can happen is they say no, putting us in the position of being right. We have the medical ship standing by..." He looked down on a board. "Yes, the Centaur, a good ship with nice nurses. It's home depot is New Sydney from Coroscate. Crew compliment seventy four point two, sixty four military medical staff under command of Captain Hindmarsh. We can send the injured back to Coroscate, and make this fight real for the Council and the Chancellor. If the dead and wounded arrive on the door step, sir, it will get the attention you want and they would have to send the men we desperately need, sir," he finished.

"Nice plan, in theory," Rockwell responded. "However, I honestly don't think even that will get them interested again. I have my orders to destroy the planet; I believe they would prefer that to sending more troops. The public do not like seeing body bags arriving on their door step from a far off planet nobody cares about any more. To the politicians, the war is over and Rriban is nothing more than inconvenience. The threat of the Dark Knights is gone; it cannot gain them popularity anymore, so it has been forgotten." Rockwell got up from the briefing table.

They were in a moderately sized room with all the commanders seated in front of the main briefing table, including Rockwell and Commander Powell. This was intended to be the briefing for all his commanders and officers, but it turned into a council of war. The General had permitted smoking, so there were slow clouds rising up from their smokes. The room grew misty as there were no windows for the smoke to escape; it just hung in the air around them. Douglas, who insisted on using an old-fashioned bamboo pipe, wore a crumpled officer's hat and never removed his shades, despite being indoors. Also in the room were Admiral William, in charge of the planet side navy, General Chester, commanders Walter, Jere, Thomas and George, and the White Knights

Ramon and Dasillo.

The two representatives of the White Knights refused to sit throughout the entire briefing, and remained standing like statues with no hint of a personality. The windowless room they were in had a low ceiling with a board on the wall behind the briefing table used to conduct intelligence briefings back when the building was in the hands of Dark Intelligence. Rockwell had relocated his main office to this building. Powell had insisted he be there as well, so they could protect him and still be seen on the lines supporting the troops. Instead of staying back letting the men do the dying, he could enjoy the comforts of safety.

"I'll offer them a forty eight hour cease fire, to recover wounded from both sides. As an added gesture, I will supply medical supplies for them to use. Commanders Walter and Jere will go. If you went, Chester, they will just shoot you. You can stay on the edge, so they can see you, but do not advance." The order was given.

Rockwell walked around the side of the room making his way to the door. He opened it quickly, flooding the room with fresh air and letting billows of smoke out of the enclosed room.

~

"Captain David, sir, they wish to talk. Look," the voice of Danielle came. Captain David, who was in charge of the gun battery, had come to the barricade to relieve the person in charge previously.

"Go get the General."

Danielle had turned to go carry out that order, and walked straight into a person wearing a black robe. The material felt soft and smooth. As Danielle stepped back and apologized, she looked up to see an empowering figure. The left arm bore the dark red arm patch of a closed fist, while the right arm was filled with kill marks from the shoulder to the cuff. Red hair was maintained down to the shoulders, and with her hands, Biaci lowered her hood.

"You need to be more aware of your surroundings; I saw them coming, Danielle. Go out to meet them and see what they want," said Biaci's stern voice. Biaci was still a teenager at heart when she first arrived, only twenty one years old. However, the days she was forced to stay here have turned the girl into a woman. Whatever Danielle saw the Emperor's Saber say to the General, it made her angrier than anyone else she had seen. Even angrier than Rockwell during the times he was hungry. She didn't hear exactly what was said because the ship had started to take off, but she could clearly see the Saber talking to the woman known as Biaci.

Danielle put the blaster rifle down, climbed up over the barricade with Captain David holding her hand for assistance. As she climbed over and back down on the other side, her face was covered in dirt and dust from the recent fighting. She didn't look pretty at all. Danielle would have killed for a bath, but ever since joining the other side, such luxuries as hot water were a thing of the past.

She walked up slowly with her hands at her sides; she knew the people coming out to meet her. In fact, she could see Commander Powell looking through his glasses, staring right at her. She could only imagine what was going through his mind right now; nothing pleasant, she was sure.

She saw Jere and smiled toward him out of habit, but got a sad look in return. As commanders Walter and Jere presented themselves and saluted, Danielle just blushed. It was commander Walter who spoke first, clearly unaware of the awkwardness between the two.

"We want a ceasefire. General Rockwell has authorized us to offer a forty-eight hour ceasefire where we can reclaim our wounded and you may do the same. Working parties of eight from each side with no weapons. As a gesture of good faith, Republic medical supplies will be left here for you to use. Any serious wounded maybe evacuated via our medical ships. However, they will be treated as prisoners of war."

"Are we at war, Commander?" Danielle replied.

"Don't be like that, Danielle. You know how things run; you served Rockwell long enough to know better," Commander Jere replied for Walter. Walter's head almost snapped backwards at this to look between Commander Jere and Danielle.

"Commander Walter, this is the former office clerk to Rockwell, Danielle. Danielle, this is Commander Walter. Despite hostilities, we must be civilized, even if you have forgotten what that means, Danielle."

11

"All these people did was steal food. General Rockwell wants to slaughter people who were starving. If you keep poking at a caged animal, eventually it will bite back. Jere.... How is Commander Eddington?" She added the last part to prove her point.

"Please, we are here to talk about the wounded and the current situation, not your personal life," remarked Walter.

"I'm not authorized to make decisions; I was sent out here to see what you want. If you are serious, you will have to come with me and speak to our General." Danielle spoke with a serious look.

"So you can take us prisoners and use us as leverage? I think not. Send someone out who can make decisions; we will wait," Walter finished ordering.

"No, wait, I will go alone. Danielle, stay here with Commander Walter and I will walk over to your lines. If anything happens to me, you will be taken prisoner. Agreed?"

She did not hesitate. She nodded, turned around, and shouted, "Commander Jere will approach to speak to the general about the wounded." With that, Jere walked off holding both arms to his sides with palms open facing them. He walked at a steady pace.

"You got a line on that man holding her?" Biaci demanded of David. For an answer, she heard the click of the single shot blaster rifle David used for accurate shooting.

"General Rockwell offers forty-eight hour ceasefire to allow both sides to collect their wounded, two work parties of eight, no weapons. We will supply medical supplies for you to use for your wounded," Commander Jere shouted.

"Get ready..." Biaci whispered. "When will the Cease fire start?" she shouted.

"If you agree to our terms, thirty minutes after we return to our lines with your response," Jere responded.

Biaci stared off into the distance, looking directly at Danielle. Too far away to speak normally, her master had explained to Biaci on the flight over how to use mental manipulation. However, she had never used it until now. Seeing the image of Danielle, she closed her mind. Mentally still seeing Danielle, she focused hard on her and started to use the dark power to send the message, "Start to walk to us slowly, get ready to run, walk to us slowly." Whenever using this, there was never a sure way to know if you got through, unless you could open your eyes like Biaci did now. She saw the shocked look on Danielle's face.

Danielle, although startled, started to walk slowly, instinctively as soon as she heard the voice in her head.

"My Lady, where…?" Commander Walter had reached out a hand to try and stop Danielle. Before he took a second step, there was a bullet sized hole in the middle of his forehead. Danielle broke off into a run as she heard a distinctive "RUN" in her head. At the same time, three men, including Captain David, had leaped over, taking Commander Jere prisoner.

"DIVE," Biaci shouted, as two shots were fired from the two tanks. Danielle dived head first into the ground as the shots flew over her head and landed behind her, bringing up earth and remains of bodies into the air, creating a perfect smoke screen to allow Danielle to get up and run for her life. She got about six paces in front of the barricade before falling forward, grasping at her right leg, screaming.

She saw Commander Powell standing next to Chester in the distance, holding a blaster rifle like Captain David's in his hand. Six men jumped over the barricade; two of them picked up Danielle under the arms and dragged her back to the barricade, while the other four held metal shields to cover their withdrawal.

Danielle, screaming bloody murder, cried out, "AHH! Biaci! Help me please!"

"Quickly get her to the storage barn! Get the doctor!" Biaci ordered. Biaci looked back out towards the Republic lines and saw them walking back towards the HQ building. The man who shot Danielle showed his frustration by snapping the blaster rifle in two over his knee and discarding the pieces on the ground. Biaci looked towards the ground.

"Stay here, Captain." She ran to the storage barn. Danielle was no longer screaming. Hopefully she had passed out, sparing herself from the pain.

Biaci slammed the doors open just in time to see the surgeon removing Danielle's right foot below the shin. She saw with disbelief that Danielle hadn't passed out, but there were tears pouring from her eyes. Danielle reached out a hand as soon as she saw Biaci enter, and Biaci rushed to her side.

"It's okay to scream, Danielle." Biaci, despite her training, had felt a connection to her, like a surrogate mother. Danielle was only eighteen, and now missing her foot.

"I'll make him pay, I swear," Biaci swore to her.

"No, I will kill him, train …OOHH!" The surgeon was tying off the end of her stub and cleaning up the wound. "Biaci please, train me I want to be like you. I want to kill them!" She had gripped Biaci's hand so hard her nails were digging into the skin, drawing blood, but Biaci didn't mind.

"How much longer?!" she turned angrily to the surgeon.

"I have to clean what is left or the infection will spread, meaning we would have to cut off even more, if it doesn't kill her," the surgeon replied in frustration. He was a well-trained medical doctor in his forties.

"Biaci!" Danielle said loudly. "Be careful whoever interrogates Jere. They have been trained to resist torture, and there is a locator chip in the back, embedded in the spine, sixth vertebrae down. I know because I had to handle the paper work for them to be issued to the General. The General made all his commanders get it for this exact reason. They will map the entire place with where you take him."

Biaci was amazed and proud how even when she was clearly in agony, she attempted to keep her mind distracted.
"I'll go sort it out now; you rest up and we will talk about training later." She kissed Danielle's blood stained hand, covered in Biaci's own blood. Biaci let go and walked out to perform her own surgery on their prisoner.

# CHAPTER 4

Large vibrations sounded throughout the ship as blaster fire was exploding all around them. Lord Duplex Agens had been using her abilities to keep them out of the range of the chasing ships. Sarah returned to the gun turrets in attempt to get some of them off their backs, but it was hopeless with the speed Duplex was flying the ship. With the speed of the ships chasing them, flown by White Knights, she was lucky if a shot got close to any of them.

"Come to the radio station! Hurry!" shouted Duplex. Sarah dropped the controls and ran to the Pilot deck. She sat down to listen to the radio station.

"Okay, do as I say!" Duplex commanded. "Turn the knob on the right ninety degrees to the right. Flip the green switch up." She turned quickly to see Sarah had followed exactly as instructed. "Good. Now on the control pad, type one, eight, zero, seven, one. Press execute." It was done; the ship started transmitting a signal outwards.

"What did I just send?" Sarah asked.

"No time to explain. Now type one, nine, eight, two, four, zero, six, and execute." Again, she turned to see that it was done. "Turn the knob on the right one hundred and eighty to the right, and press three, one, three, and press execute and transmit. Then come up to the front."

Sarah, following her instructions, got up to move up front. As she sat back down in the co-pilot seat, the screen display turned black with a picture of a white hand, similar to the one on Duplex's arm patch.

"Sarah, speak. Tell them," Duplex said as she turned.

"Tell them what, Duplex?" Sarah replied, not fully understanding.

"Tell the Emperor who you are and why you are here!" An anxious expression spread over the Saber's face. Realization dawning on Sarah, she snapped to attention. "My Emperor, I am Sarah from Rriban, part of the rear guard to protect your forces as they withdrew. We are still alive and hold out in a district on Rriban. We are fighting and have taken control of the district. We wanted to welcome you to a liberated Rriban, but we are fighting broomsticks with knifes against blaster rifles. With your Saber and Biaci, they have started the fight on Rriban. The Republic doesn't have enough men to hold the planet. If we try to take over the planet, the General Rockwell has orders to destroy the planet." She looked at Duplex after she had finished as no response came back.

"Saber, your apprentice is where?" the Emperor's creepy voice finally responded.

"She is on Rriban. They needed a general to lead them, as you predicted; she is leading us back to Rriban, my Emperor. I had to fly out to get word back to the Empire, however, we are being chased by a White Knight Dreadnaught. I did not want to lead them to Kaas, so I got within range of transmission and headed off in another direction."

"Let go of your controls!" the Emperor commanded Duplex, who obeyed instantly. "I have a surprise for you, Saber." The ship, while still in a jump, turned to the right by itself. With a flash and a sudden jolt, the communication with the Emperor ended. At the same time their ship came out of the jump, ahead of them was a flotilla of Dark Imperial ships, The Morgan Rice and Dragomire.

As soon as Duplex's ship came out of the jump, sixteen Dark Imperial fighters flew past them, entangling themselves with the White Knight fighters. The Dragomire rushed forward at full speed as Duplex hit the thrusters, heading for the docking bay.

The White Knight Dreadnaught came out of the jump and started firing instantly as it came under fire from the Morgan Rice and Dragomire.

On the bridge of the Dragomire, the Admiral, in his fifties, acted like a kid again, excited by the chance of battle. This was their first chance of revenge since they were expelled to Kaas City.

"Bring all guns to bare," Dark Admiral Takeo shouted. The full space battle erupted and the White Knight dreadnaught appeared to have launched every single space craft it had.

The Morgan Rice got a shot off on the right side, just below the communications signals.

"White Knight. Damn it, fire again! Keep jamming, keep jamming!" Soemu, the Dark Admiral of the Morgan Rice, shouted. He was forty five and a veteran of the last conflict.

"We cannot let them send off long range transmissions. Hold until I say!" he bellowed the order.

"Guns and missiles loaded sir!" said one of Soemu's bridge officers.

"FIRE! Quickly fire!" Soemu shouted as the White Knight ship started to turn.

On the bridge of the White Knight Dreadnaught, it was Master Sergio's turn to use some of their skill.

"Get ready please for maneuver Phoenix Beta… Proceed," Master Sergio ordered. The White Knight ship shook as the blasts from the Morgan Rice hit.

"Communications are out!" Master Sergio's squire announced.

"Proceed with the maneuver," Sergio repeated. The Ship flew between the two Dark Knight ships making it impossible for them to fire without hitting the other. As it passed the ends of the Dark Dreadnaughts, the full array of guns and missiles on both sides fired, knocking out the engines of both the Morgan Rice and Dragomire.

Sergio's ship performed a one hundred eighty degree turn and proceeded back up between the two, shooting up both ships as they passed. At the end, the ship made the jump, leaving the Dark Knights looking at the smoke trail of where Sergio had been.

"COWARDS!" shouted Takeo. "Damage report!" he demanded.

"Sir!" Bollinger replied. "Engines disabled, minor damage to the starboard, docking bays four and six took hits, our fighters still engaged. They left their fighters behind, they abandoned them. Should we take prisoners?"

"Emperor's orders are to kill all; no prisoners!" Duplex reported as she entered the bridge.

"You heard the Emperor's Saber," an annoyed Takeo said, looking at Bollinger as he got up.

"My Lady, perhaps you could tell us why we are here?" he asked with no trace of aggression; all anger seemed gone.

"Admiral, this is Sarah. She is of the Rear Guard that was left behind on Rriban eight years ago. Today, they are fighting to liberate the planet and they need our help. Admiral, we are going back to Rriban." Duplex couldn't help smiling.

The Admiral was too astonished looking at the uniform Sarah was now wearing; Sarah, knowing the plan, had put her old uniform on the ship ahead of time. For being a part of the rear guard, they had been awarded a very unique custom badge. It was a circular badge, worn on the right shoulder, with the Dark Knight's symbol in the middle. The word "Consequia" was written across the top, with "Rriban" along the bottom, roughly translating to Rear Guard Rriban, or Rriban's Rear Guard.

No one from the Rear Guard made it back to Kaas City for obvious reasons. When the Admiral saw the uniform, he felt humbled as honor mandated. He stood to attention and saluted Sarah, who was only the rank of a Dark Captain, while he was an Admiral.

"Bridge stand too! Officer on deck. Consequia," Admiral Takeo shouted. The entire bridge staff stood about face, all stopping what they were doing, and either saluted or stood to attention.

"Please, Captain Sarah, take my seat for a moment." He directed her to the chair, accompanied by Duplex Agens. As Sarah sat down, the Admiral issued an order to the ship's captain; he turned on the ship's intercom and video feed.

"Crew of the Dragomire, I have an important announcement. Captain, please transmit this over to the Morgan Rice, highest priority." He waited a few moments for the order to be carried out and for the normal tell-tale sign the call was put through.

"The Dark Empire has committed a grave injustice. We have assumed too much that our old home world was lost to the enemy. I, too, until today, believed this. However, I just learned different. Sitting in my chair is a member of the Consequia of Rriban, only those who were there got this badge. Today, she is here. Today, I learned they have suffered because they stayed loyal to us. They are now fighting to liberate Rriban. You all wanted to know what we were doing here, why we were waiting. Now you have your answer. We are going home. Let us get the engines fixed, and then on to Rriban. Admiral Soemu, please, if you would, bring yourself and officer staff to my ship for a conference with the Emperor's Saber. We are going to war! Today, we are going home!" He finished announcing and the huge uproar of emotion could be heard from the entire Dragomire crew, as well as the Morgan Rice crew through the communication system.

# CHAPTER 4.2

"Initiate combat procedures; bring the city to a ready state. Conflict procedures, guards at all sensitive areas," ordered Sweeper, pacing the floor as she looked up and down the display panels watching her Readers work.

"People of the Dark Intelligence," Sweeper started to announce. "I have received word from Dragomire; the Emperor's Saber is on board with a member of Rriban's Consequia, and entered into combat with the White Knights and the Republic. Put the Dark Empire onto a war footing."

It was done as soon as she gave the order. The switches were flipped, and orders from the Readers were read out to the various Cryptic Agents out in the field. The door opened up and six Dark Guards entered, led in by Captain Tyrik.

"It is good to see you, Ma'am. Reporting for duty, we are your guard." He began pointing at random spots and the guards spread out to each spot he pointed.

"After the events of the Civil War and the nature of your work that goes on here, we have been ordered to place a guard. When your order went out to place guards, that includes you now." He looked at her with a smile.

"Very well, if we are stuck with each other, just don't get in my way," she said with no trace of a smile.

"No Ma'am, you have my men and I am to be your own personal guard." He saw she was about to protest. "Emperor's orders, ma'am. There is four Dark Knights guarding your entrance. We replaced your man at the desk; he did not pose a very intimidating threat to anyone wanting to do harm. Ma'am, may we withdraw to your office? I have more sensitive information from the Dark Council to pass on." He stood perfectly to attention.

Sweeper looked at him and decided to make him wait a little. "Readers, situation report? Reader four, initiate a lockdown on the spaceport. No flights may leave or enter unless military and have written orders."

"Yes ma'am," Reader four instantly replied.

"Ma'am, all instructions have been executed. Kaas City is mobilized; they've doubled the guard around Cryptic M's statue." Reader Eight turned to look at Sweeper. In turn, she looked toward Tyrik, who gestured to her office.

"Shall we, ma'am?" he said, suppressing a smile.

"Fine. Reader Eight, you are in charge. If any more news come from the front lines, alert me." With that said, she turned on the spot and walked through the conference hall into her office.

"You have to forgive me, Tyrik," she said as she approached her desk. "I cannot be seen to be too familiar with you in front of my people here. They will get the wrong idea." She sat down facing him.

"The wrong idea? Like that you are a wild woman that likes to have fun, instead of being round up tight-ass until you snap again?" He walked over to the desk, but didn't sit. "I can see why you want to hide that. It would ruin your reputation that you actually have a personality."

"To business, Captain, we are in a state of war. Peace time luxuries have to be put on hold… You really think we are going back to Rriban?"
She looked up at the captain.

"Not at liberty to say. However, having met the Emperor's Saber and seeing what she has done, I would not be surprised if she sacked Coroscate… Ma'am, I wish I could say me being here was my doing, however, I was ordered here. The Emperor is concerned about the Dark Empire Intelligence; he believes Intelligence to be compromised. We replaced your security guard because he allowed Lord Thant enter without a pass card. When you were… you were engaged in other matters." He winked at Sweeper and she acknowledged the courtesy with a nod to signal she understood.

"I do not know why we have been ordered to double the guard for the statue. However, I have been ordered to ask; did you place anything on the Statue recently?"

Sweeper thought back, "Yes, I placed my Reader name plate on the day of his anniversary, that same day you and I met."

"No one else was with you at the time?" He asked.

"I cannot divulge that information, I've been ordered by our mutual boss," she said with a serious look.

"You just did, you just did answer… so the problem is, ma'am, between the day you placed the item on the statue and now, the Statue was tampered with. So right now you are a suspect. However, there is no evidence to suggest you did anything. So…"

"So what you are telling me is you are here not so much to protect us, than to watch me, to make sure I am not a traitor?" she interrupted.

"I'm sure you have nothing to worry about. If you did nothing wrong, then there should be no problem. You won't even notice me or my men. I am going to guard you just as well as I did Lord Chakû," he finished proudly.

"Really, Captain? Remind me, where is Lord Chakû? I have not seen him in quite a long time." She stood up looking mad. "Was it the Dark Council or the Emperor who ordered this?"

"Like you said, Ma'am, our mutual boss," he replied with a sad expression.

"If it is not you, and I am sure you are not guilty, then it is good I am here because it means someone else is guilty and is actively against us, and they have access to the Intelligence with Sweeper's codes. Oh yes, that is the other thing. All your codes have been changed; you will be allowed to log in one time with your current information, then they will stop working. You will have access to the next codes that will be listed on the display… Now, I'll return to duty. It doesn't look too well if a guard stays alone with Sweeper too long, does it?" He winked as he left the office.

Sweeper was furious at the situation, being under the suspicion of being a traitor. After everything she had personally done, no time for that now. The war must take priority.

She leaned over and entered her old code for the last time. It came on fine, and the list of codes was displayed. She memorized them, then removed the file. She flipped the switch.

"Priority call code: Yellow, Delta, Alpha, Romeo, Kilo. Transmit," she announced. Again, the call was placed and the collective display of the Dark Council members appeared; all six of them, stood as mini figures on the screen.

"My Lords, initiate plan Ban as instructed for this situation. I hear by announce, The Dark Empire is at war with the Republic and the White Knights. Situation report: space battle with the forces of the Dark Military and the White Knights. Present, Dragomire and the Morgan Rice. Also, My Lords, The Emperor's Saber and a Rear Guard of Rriban, I say again Rriban." She was interrupted mid-way.

"Be very sure of what you are saying, Sweeper." A sly voice spoke out loud.

"The Dark Dreadnaughts were disabled by the White Knight Super Dreadnaught and fled the scene, abandoning its fighters. The Admirals accompanied by the Saber and Captain Sarah, they are conducting a war council before launching the attack on Rriban." She continued as if not interrupted at all. I have ordered an Intelligence scout ship to follow the Dreadnaught to maintain cover. They last transmitted before going out of range, they are on task.

According to Plan Ban instructions, The Dark Council was not informed of this on the orders of the Emperor. Only now, after the situation has been declared, were you to be informed. My Lords may our power shine through!" and she ended the call.

That felt great and she giggled to herself; she was in charge of them for once and it felt incredible.

"Ma'am!" Reader four shouted. "Ma'am, come quick!"
Sweeper stood up and ran back out towards the shouts of Reader four.

"What is it? What is the problem? ...OH!" She was stunned into silence.

# CHAPTER 6

"Leave us!" Biaci shouted as the door opened. The room they were in was completely dark with a strong stench of urine; Biaci stood in the doorway silhouetted by the light outside.

"But...?" the Dark Captain Jack was about to question.

"...L.E.A.V.E," Biaci said with a slow angry voice, full of venom. Captain Jack had only known Biaci since the day she landed on Rriban, he'd never seen anyone as furious as Biaci was now; it actually scared him slightly. Without hesitation, he got up and looked at Commander Jere.

"I wouldn't want to be you right now." He left as Biaci moved out of the way, letting him pass. She walked in and closed the door, barring it with the wooden plank that was standing against the wall by the door.

"Please, how is Danielle? I don't care what you do to me, just tell me Danielle is okay." The pleading question went unanswered. Biaci slowly walked up to him and traced her finger down his chest all the way to his crotch. She walked around behind Commander Jere and traced her finger from his bottom up to the base of his neck. She stopped for a moment, then traced back down his spine, stopping on the place Danielle had warned her about, the sixth vertebra down.

"Please, how is she? I will knock all of Powell's teeth out." No sign of a struggle. She walked round again, now facing him. Hate dripped out of every pore of her body.

"Danielle warned me of you. I know about your locator device, that you are trained to resist torture." She looked at him. He stayed silent.

"There is no point staying silent. I know it is there; I can just remove it myself now, leaving you a cripple. You had no plans for the future, right?" She continued to stare at him. "Why all the concern about Danielle?"

"We were to be married. We been together for six years; we wanted to wait until we were off world. Then she joined you lot," he said.

"Our lot? Our lot?! It may surprise you, Commander, however, your Republic is the aggressor here. You came onto our planet; it is you that started to starve the people here. They always were going to fight. These people would never have just died out without making the Republic pay for it." She about turned and walked over to a table with several instruments laid out neatly to be used on Commander Jere. "Your wedding may be off. Danielle lost her right foot. She wants to kill Powell."

"NO! You can't let her; that is not Danielle," he interrupted. She spun around fast, walked over to him, and rubbed the side of his face with her hand gently.

"Why is it men always believe they need to protect us women? Danielle is not the woman you knew anymore, it would seem. She has already killed some of your men, so it isn't like she isn't capable. In fact, I would say it was you that needs protecting....Don't worry, Commander, I'm here. Don't you find me attractive?"

He did. She had the figure of a well-built woman with light red colored skin and red hair down to her shoulders. The robe she was wearing highlighted all her womanly features. He looked down at Biaci's body and got aroused.

"Ah, that is a good boy. I see you do." She smiled. "You have been trained to resist torture..." She grabbed hold of the commander's testicles and started to squeeze. "But why does this have to be like that, when you could have a nice time and get this unpleasantness over with?" She started stroking the Commander's penis now slowly.

"Commander," she said in a flirty voice. "Tell me you know how to turn off that locator, because I know you do." The commander remained silent.

"Oh dear." With the hilt of her saber, she slammed it up into the Commander's scrotum. He let out a scream of pain, and Biaci instantly grabbed his throat.

"NO! You do not get to scream. Your 'fiancée' is over there in pure agony and refused to scream as her foot was removed." Biaci raised her hand, revealing the hand covered in blood. "She gripped tight onto me and kept focus rather than scream, so you will not scream. Do so again and I will gag you with your own penis." She let go of his throat.

"The only way to disable it is to remove it surgically. It cannot be disabled while in me, not even if you kill me. It was designed so they could always find my body," he managed to say, breathing heavily.

"So it can be removed?" She started stroking his penis again, and again, he was aroused. He didn't speak. "Come on, Commander, you cannot tell me you don't like this. How can it be removed?" She gave a tiny little lick on the end of his penis. "It can get even better if you just tell me."

"Err... by oo... going in from the side, right hand side, underneath the arm. They put us to sleep and inserted a probe. Just look, you will see the circle scar." She got up, felt the skin just below his right arm, and indeed, her fingers grazed the rough skin of the scar.

She walked over to the table, about to select a knife, when a loud bang knocked on the door. "Biaci, Biaci! It is me, let me in. It's Danielle."

This surprised Biaci. She immediately walked over, removed the bar, and opened the door to see Danielle on makeshift crutches. She hobbled in, and Biaci closed and locked the door behind her.

"You may not want to be here, Danielle," Biaci said directly to her.

"Apparently, he told me you and him were together. If this is true, you will not want to be here for this."

"I had to be here." She looked at him, clearly seeing what Biaci had been doing. "It's okay, Biaci; I would of done the same. If someone has to do it, I want it to be me." She hopped over to Jere and looked at him as he was tied up. "She kissed him softly and kneed him hard in the groin. "You told her to go in under the arm, didn't you?"

"Danielle, no, what are you doing?" Jere asked desperately in a painful voice. Danielle backed up and looked away towards Biaci.

"If you went in where he told you, it would of set off the self-destruct, killing you both. I saw how they inserted them; if you summon the doctor, I can explain the procedure and have him reverse it."

Biaci stepped forward. "Do you want to save him?" She placed her left hand on Danielle's shoulder.

"He would be useful to you. He is General Rockwell's son," she said, looking down.

"NO! Danielle, what have they done to you?!" Jere shouted. Biaci looked towards the commander, but was then forced to look back at Danielle. She suddenly dropped the crutches, grabbed Biaci, and kissed her fully on the mouth, holding her very tenderly. Biaci kissed back, too stunned to do otherwise. As Danielle looked directly at Biaci, she kept glancing towards the commander, so Biaci could understand what she was doing. Biaci understood and played along. She held Danielle's back very tenderly, while Danielle started to hold onto her ass. Danielle then grabbed her breasts, squeezing them. Just before Danielle carried on, she spoke to Jere, "I guess you would like to be here." She gave him a wink, then rubbed her face in Biaci's chest.

Danielle started to go down to a knee with Biaci's helping hand. Danielle noticed it had done the trick, that flirting with Biaci had aroused Jere yet again. Danielle picked up one of the crutches and slammed it hard up between his legs, drawing blood. They could hear bone breaking as he passed out.

"I want nothing to do with the Republic anymore, and I want nothing to do with Rockwell anymore. Looking at you reminds me of him, and you are just as easy to manipulate and twist to do what we want," she spat at Jere.

She turned to Biaci. "I pledge to honor and serve the Dark Empire and I pledge to serve you, to train  to be stronger than you, to learn all that I can from you as a Dark Knight; I want to be your apprentice." She bowed her head and remained silent.

Biaci didn't respond. She walked over to the commander and lifted his head up to look closely at his face, confirming what Danielle said about seeing the resemblance to Rockwell. She walked back over to Danielle.

"I hereby accept your pledge into the Dark Empire, and I am seriously impressed with your repressed anger and power you display. To say you impressed me is understatement. Looking at you, no one would ever think you were with them. I want an apprentice like you. How would you train with one foot?" she said with a serious look towards Danielle.

"Accept me as an apprentice, my master, and I will tell all, the Republic has all we need and we have what they want. Look at Jere," she said, looking up to Biaci with a beseeching gaze.

"Very well. Who you once were, you are no more. Your passion gives you strength. The life you are leaving dies with your betrayal of your beloved. Rise Fortis and take your place by my side." Biaci stepped back, not offering any assistance now.

On one foot alone, she stood up and balanced without any crutches.

"Thank you, my master." She hopped while keeping her balance; after a long while, she was standing on one foot next to Biaci, just one pace behind her.

"Enough of this," Biaci remarked. Using the dark power, she lifted the crutches, and they flew under both of Fortis' arms.

"Now, tell me, apprentice," she ordered.

"Yes, master, but first." She turned, removed the plank from the door and opened it, revealing the doctor who operated on her just moments earlier.

"How much did you hear?" Biaci demanded.

"All of it." He went over to the commander. "Apprentice, come here. I will need you to explain exactly, so you need to be watching over me." The doctor knelt down and opened his bag of surgical tools. Fortis went around behind him and held her finger at the point of the sixth vertebra. With her right index finger, she traced a line to the side Commander Jere had spoken of to Biaci. She moved her left hand down two vertebrae and fourteen inches to the left.

"Enter here, Doctor. The detonator is here." She pointed to the right shoulder blade. "The whole device is no bigger than your little finger, just comes with lots of attachments. Master, we may need you to make sure it doesn't go off with your Dark power."

"AHHHHH," Jere suddenly screamed as the doctor started to cut into him.

"Shut him up, unless you want a cripple," the agitated doctor demanded. Biaci walked over to him quickly.

"Relax, Commander, when you wake up you'll be a liberated person, out from the control of your dad and the Republic. You will get to experience what it is like to us, free." She punched him hard in the face, certain she broke his nose knocking him out again.

"Apprentice, tell me now, while you are helping the doctor, what is your plan?" she ordered.

"Yes, master. Well, it's simple to use him, of course. The Republic ship Centaur is planet side from Coroscate. It has everything we need and we have what they want. I intend to use him and this is how..." she explained, as she pointed to the next insertion point for the doctor.

~

"How DARE YOU!" shouted Rockwell as he rubbed the bruised knuckles of his right fist. He had just punched Commander Powell. Powell was lying flat on his back, face filled with stark shock and surprise that his General laid a hand on him. He felt the side of his face, checking for blood with his left hand, and looked amazed at his general.

"They have my son, and you go and shoot that girl, which endangered his life by your action of trying to shoot that girl. If you had killed her, instead of a happy cheering crowd, you would of turned them into a vengeful army, and who do you think they will take their revenge on?" Rockwell said as he turned with his hands behind his back.

"You are hereby transferred to the Centaur; I do not want you in my command. You will be the target of their hate; everyone around you is not safe. NOW GET OUT!" Rockwell ordered.

Powell looked like he wanted to protest, but Commander Douglas gave him a stern look. When he looked to Chester for assistance, he was again surprised to see him pointing to the door. Commander Powell picked himself up off the ground.

"Fine, I'll go. You can blame me all you want. It is your own fault, you pompous idiot. You created this situation by sticking your head in the ground," he retorted.

"Commander Douglas, please see that Lieutenant Powell makes it to the hospital ship. He is not allowed off that ship; if he sets foot on Rriban again, he will be arrested. Make sure he understands." Rockwell continued looking out the windows as he gave the order, completely ignoring the now Lt. Powell.

"Sir!" Douglas replied as he turned around and took Powell by the arm. Douglas pointed to two foot soldiers to help escort Powell away.

"I know the way," Lt Powell responded angrily, jerking away from Commander Douglas' hand.

"Sir", General Chester, acting Commander, spoke, "The locator is active; your son is alive still. They have him in one building. They have not moved him, however he is alive."

"All that means is they haven't killed him yet," Rockwell said with a heavy sigh. "We still have what is left of the wounded out there, however I think we have to forget about them. And now they have my son prisoner and I fear I will have to forget about him too. His mother will divorce me; she pleaded to me to get him out of the army, but he wanted to go. I either let him join up or he was going to do it behind our backs." He solemnly looked towards Chester.

"General, what would you do?" Rockwell asked, paying him the respect of referring to his proper rank.

"Are you asking as a father or a General? Because depending which you are asking as, there is totally different answers. As a father, you are not going to like the general's response." He looked directly at Rockwell.

"As a General, Chester. The Republic first, personal life second," he said very quietly, not sounding convincing at all.

"Very well, General Rockwell. Your son is expendable; he is just one man and we have already lost hundreds of men. When our forces are limited already, doing anything to try and get him back puts him in jeopardy. It also puts our entire mission in jeopardy. It will be best if you presume he is already dead, because soon as we do anything, he will be dead.

Even if you would threaten to start setting off the charges, they would ignore that because even if they complied, they would know you would use the same threat every time to get what you want. So they will never comply to such demands as, 'Give me my son or I start destroying the city.'" He paused and turned to look out the window alongside the silently crying Rockwell. As a courtesy, he ignored the crying and continued.

"I know, Rockwell, it is the sons that are supposed to cremate their fathers, not the other way round. You have my regrets, however you really cannot do anything, but wait to see what they want. Keep up a strong appearance. Display the armor units instead of the men up front; make them fear we will start to shell them, but do not fire until we hear from them first. Because if we act first, he is dead for sure, and the only chance of seeing him alive again is to see what they want."

Rockwell did not respond at first. He walked over to a wall cabinet and opened it to pull out a bottle and two glasses. He removed the stopper and poured the contents into the two glasses. He took one of them, quickly downed the entire contents, and then refilled the glass.
He put the stopper back in the bottle, placed it back in the cabinet, and closed the cabinet door again.

"Officers are not supposed to drink on duty, General, however given the circumstances..." Rockwell was interrupted.

"Forgive me, General. Damn the regulations," he states as he accepted the glass of Coroscate Brandy and they started to drink.

"To the memory of Commander Jere," Rockwell toasted.

# CHAPTER 7

"The situation is this," Sarah began. Duplex let Sarah do most of the talking, as she really drove the point home and the Admirals were much more impressed. "Since the military left and we guarded the withdraw, The Republic gave us a choice to either join them or stay out of the Republic. We stayed loyal to the empire, expecting you to come. With the Emperor's Saber's arrival with her apprentice, we have the chance to liberate ourselves. They have a small garrison of thirty thousand men. They pulled all their non-combatants to fight too. Supply clerks, anyone that was not meant to fight, they put a gun in their hands because they are afraid of us."

"When we left, we had obtained two Republic tanks and barricaded the district south of the former intelligence building. We have double the personnel, however, no mass organization, and the only weapons we have is what we take from the enemy, which was eight rifles and two tanks and what look like a gun battery." Sarah looked towards Duplex as she sat down.

"Admirals, spirited as Sarah is, the situation is that the once strong Rear Guard had almost ten years between the loss of Rriban until now. They became relaxed and lost some of their edge they once had. Before we left, they had started training again. So, although we have more personnel, it is still effectively an army versus an armed resistance. Without our help, they will be crushed. We do have a real chance of liberating the planet," Duplex stated.

"I appreciate all you have gone through, Captain," remarked Admiral Soemu. "However, we need to look at the overall picture here. Can we safely liberate the planet and hold it? It does no good just to re-capture the planet to just lose it again." He looked to his fellow Admiral.

"When we go to Rriban, how do you intend to stop General Rockwell from setting off the charges? Otherwise, all of this is academic. We could land, pull everyone out, and retire. However, then it will leave the Republic knowing we are alive and will start to hunt us. So if we go, it has to be to stay or die. However, unless you have an answer for the explosives, there really is not much we can do. Also, we have lost the element of surprise. That White Knight ship will have alerted the garrison on Rriban that we are coming," Admiral Takeo commented, looking directly at the Saber, completely ignoring Soemu, though his answer indirectly answered Soemu's protest.

"They know we saw where the explosives are placed. He will only set off the explosives if he is in danger of losing the planet. So we need to maintain the illusion for them of that, of a winning position until the very end. Also, there is also a more serious concern; I must stress this meeting must not be repeated or transmitted back to the Empire. Someone from the Empire is working with the enemy. I will transmit everything said here directly to the Emperor and he will relay to whom he chooses." The Saber glanced at both Admirals with a serious look.

"I already transmitted a situation report to Intelligence; they will know by now you are here," Admiral Soemu reported.

"That is fine, just do not send anything else unless you check with Admiral Takeo or myself," the Saber ordered.

Duplex, suddenly feeling a weight or pressure coming on top of her, bowed her head, taking in what was like an incoming message. She had not felt anything from a force bond this strong for a long time, since Lord Chakû was still alive. However, this was coming from her apprentice, Biaci. She felt the anxiety and fury that was unprecedented for Biaci. Duplex then felt the power radiate from Biaci as it was channeled through this force channel.

A soft hand rested on Duplex Agens' right forearm, which did the trick, snapping Duplex out of her trance. She shook her head and opened her eyes to see the conference room once again. It was a grey room with black trim around the middle. The table could seat twelve, but just the four of them were sealed in the room, facing each other. Admiral Takeo forwent the formality of sitting at the end of the table even though they were on his ship.

"Thank you," Duplex said quietly. Admiral Soemu mistook this as a sign of her being exhausted, while Takeo instantly poured her a glass of water and placed it in front of her.

"We can continue this once we have a more stable plan; we have the engines to get repaired. The scout ships sent to chase the White Knight ship should be reporting back in anytime now." Admiral Takeo stood up, headed to the door, and paused. "Oh, see the quartermaster and they will show you to your quest quarters," he said, then he left followed by Soemu.

Standing outside, Admiral Takeo pulled out a cigar and paused to light it as he looked towards Soemu. "Impressions?" he asked.

"If I told you my impressions, I could be seen as a traitor. I would of called anyone else crazy, ordering them to the ships doctor to be looked at if it wasn't for that patch on her arm," he replied.

"Yes, they do tend to appear as a certified lunatic. I would think so too if I had not seen her at work. I was on the Bridge as I saw the Turned crash into the Desired, seeing how one Dark Knight had manipulated the Dark Council members to look like nothing other than scared boys. Then seeing her fight after I landed planet side, after they had destroyed the gun turrets, causing severe damage to the Dragomire. I will never doubt them, or more accurately, I will never doubt her. She is the Saber of Kaas and she earned that title." After few chokes on his cigar, he saluted goodnight to Soemu and headed off towards his bridge while Soemu went to return to his ship.

"What was that?" Sarah had a concerned look on her face, waiting for Duplex to recover herself.

"It is nothing; it took me by surprise. I won't be caught off guard again. I am apparently more connected to my Apprentice, your sister, than I realized." She looked towards Sarah. "Sometimes we can filter the strong emotions we feel and send them to each other. This can be good or bad, perhaps even very bad. I had a bond with my master that was strong. I had one too with your brother, but it was not quite as strong. This was something else. Whatever is going on, your sister is extremely angry. That is what I felt, pure unadulterated fury, then the power. The Emperor saw this, saw she could lead us back to Rriban, it is just...." She trailed off into thought.

"Just what...?" Sarah asked.

"She has become a master; there can only be one master, one apprentice, so it means the next time we see each other, we have to fight," she said, still looking at Sarah. Sarah instinctively let go of Duplex's arm, shocked as she knew what Duplex had meant.

34

"You said the Emperor predicted this?" Sarah asked. "So that means he had to of seen this too. Go report to him; you have done a lot for the Empire already, it seems. I think you've earned enough to ask for a favor or something," Sarah pleaded.

"I will go and report, but I will not mention this, other than what I have felt." She stood up. "However, this means I need to look for a new apprentice. Keep in mind, Sarah, as you already know, your brother and your sister have the power, which means you do too. It is why you survived I'm sure of it," Duplex pointed out to Sarah.

"I know what you are driving at; I prefer the way I am, thank you. It is handy to have the extra boost here and there, however, the Empire needs people like me in the military or it would just fall apart," Sarah responded, smiling at Duplex.

Duplex had just gotten to the door as it opened, and Sarah had just stood up, finishing the glass of water, when the siren sounded. The intercom came on, and the voice of the Dragomire's captain, Captain Mike, rang out, "All hands, General quarters, man your stations. Emperor's Saber to the Bridge. This is NOT a drill. All hands, man your stations."

~

Deep in space, under the cover of stealth, the two scout ships that followed the White Knight Dreadnaught had come out of the jump and remained still, observing the ship. It had to stop short of Rriban due to the damage it sustained. It had been too close to do another jump, however it was clear it came out of the jump way too early.

The first scout ship was crewed by a crew of four. They were cramped, as the arrangement was not meant for comfort, however the crew could stay stationary in space for quite some time.

The second scout ship had a compliment of forty eight and the capacity to perform stealth surgical strikes.

The White Knight Dreadnaught had come out of the jump and disengaged it's weapons and defenses, making it a very tempting target. The ship was proceeding at half speed towards Rriban.

The enemy was too close for the scout ships to risk talking to each other. Therefore, the small craft that was only able to observe, was forced to watch as their partner started to proceed forward.

Apparently, the target of an unguarded dreadnaught was too tempting. The Captain of the larger scout ship, Captain Philip, was looking at the screen and could see the sensitive spot of the ship. A missile up the engine exhaust led to the 'sweet spot,' where most ships would be disabled when they had shields up, if they took a hit. However, with shields down, the direct hit would destroy the Dreadnaught with a single hit.

"Silent! Not a single word. I just want to return the favor they did to us." He leaned forward and gripped the armrest of his chair, leaning to the right and forward. Apparently the suspense was getting to the Captain. He was in his forties, wearing glasses, and black short hair, and his uniform shirt was pressed nicely as if it had just been issued to him.

"Get ready to lower the stealth and fire on my command." He paused as he started to tap with his left hand on the armrest to count down. Tap Eight, Tap Seven, Tap Six, Tap-...

"CAPTAIN!" shouted the crew member on the captains left. Lt Paul shouted, but it was too late. Six White Knight Ships had formed round them and fired directly at the ship's engines, disabling the scout ship. They fired several more shots.

"Relax!" Captain Philip ordered. "Clearly they are not going to kill us or we wouldn't be here still."

Their displays went black, then smashed, as steam bellowed out and the ship took another small hit. "Ship hull at twenty five percent, Captain. She won't take another hit; weapons are gone, engines destroyed." Lt. Paul was looking for the captain to pull a miracle.

Over the ship's communicator, the voice of a White Knight became very loud. "Dark Knight vessel, you have ten minutes to abandon ship before we destroy you. De-cloak and abandon ship."

"Transmit the surrender, Lieutenant. Then do as requested," the Captain said solemnly.

Being this was not a normal ship that had escape pods, each member of the ship was already seated in their own escape seat. They pushed the buttons and a cylinder surrounded each of them, each with an individual rebreather mask. The floor under them opened up and all the crew members were gone except for the Captain.

He waited to make sure his crew were safely away before he destroyed the ship with him aboard.

The resulting explosion disabled four and destroyed two of the White Knight ships. The small observation scout ship could do nothing, but just sit and watch it all. To make sure they were not detected, they turned all power off and were on their masks and using heavy winter gear to protect themselves from the cold.

They observed what looked like forty survivors from the scout ship. The White Knight Dreadnaught had stopped and started recovery operations using the tractor beams. They could of easily picked up the crew with the two ships, however, they must of sustained damage from the explosion as they returned to the Dreadnaught.

It was then that the crew member on the scout ship took a chance. They sent and fired an emergency transponder pod back to the empire fleet. It paid off between the ships going back and the Dreadnaught focused on the survivors' pods. They would not and didn't notice the pod being sent off. Even if they had, they would of assumed it was from one of the survivors.

The White Knights now had prisoners and there was nothing the Empire could do about it, except take turns and go to sleep to conserve oxygen on their masks.

# CHAPTER 8

"Commander Chester! Sir, the enemy is flagging us," one of the Republic soldiers on the lines shouted.

Commander Chester came running down ahead of the armored tanks looking through his glasses.

"The Enemy is going to be sending a message alert, General Rockwell. Give him my compliments and ask he join me presently, on the double." He looked back at the soldier.

"Move!" he shouted as he watched the soldier run off to fetch the General.

He pulled out the display and saw Commander Jere's signal had moved, and apparently, was now at their barricade. He saw it move about slightly, then horror struck his face. At the same time the blast of the tank fired, he saw the locator signal flying across the screen towards them. Then he looked up into the sky to see a small bundle flying across the sky.

"What is it, General Chester?" Rockwell asked, as he joined him on the line. He looked up at the flying package in the sky as it landed a few yards in front of their troops. A ground trooper rushed down to it, picked it up and ran the package up to the acting Commander, General Chester.

"General, the enemy has sent us a message," the trooper stated, taking note of the bloody mess. They opened it, and General Rockwell looked like he might faint when he saw the locator chip covered in blood, knowing it was Jere's blood, his son's blood.

Chester, however, picked up the notes. There was one small piece with huge writing simply saying, 'Look at our lines.' Doing so, he picked up his glasses and saw Commander Jere. "He's alive, Sir!" Chester shouted.

General Rockwell snapped forward, as if he were on a spring, and picked up his glasses, "He looks hurt!"

Chester looked down at the main message, and it read,

> *"To the leading officers of the Republic Occupation Force, we will accept the forty eight hour ceasefire you offered to extract the wounded, with additional conditions. We want the water back on for the duration of the ceasefire. We also will need medical supplies, droids. Those that are too heavily wounded, we will consent to be taken to your hospital ship. We demand we escort our wounded all the way to the ship, as an insurance to the fact they make it to the ship alive and not executed, as your previous example by your officer demonstrated.*
>
> *One of the wounded will require surgery aboard your hospital ship, we want that person returned. At the end of the ceasefire, your son will be returned. Two work parties, unarmed, will be allowed to recover any wounded and cremate the dead. The people escorting the wounded to your ship will be unarmed, and if not returned, your son dies.*
>
> *You can use your son's locator chip to fire your reply back to us. Your son's wellbeing is up to you.*
>
> *Signed, Dark Knight Master Biaci"*

"They want the ceasefire with some modifications to the demands." He handed the piece of paper, flapping in the wind, over to General Rockwell. Rockwell just looked at the paper, but didn't take it.

"You are hereby in charge of the forces for the duration of the negotiations of this ceasefire. I cannot trust myself to make the right decision any more, General, not with my son involved. Do what you must." He briefly looked up at Chester, then back out to the enemy, and walked slowly back towards the HQ building. As he did, Commander Douglas saluted.

"Sir! Orders?" He turned, looked, and watched him walk away slowly, not stopping to look at the commander. Rockwell just kept his head down.

"General Chester is in command for now," he said quietly and continued walking away.

Douglas, puzzled, proceeded to Chester and saluted, "Sir, what is wrong with the General?"

"Commander Rockwell put me charge for these negotiations; they have added some conditions to the ceasefire." He looked towards a Republic signal man. "You there, signal 'we want time to consider their message.'" He waited for the man with the flash light to transmit the message and for the response to be decoded.

"They give us one hour, sir," the soldier replied.

Admiral William came running, followed by the Medical doctor.

"General, sir!" William shouted.

"What is it, Admiral?" Chester looked up at William.

"Acting-Commander Rockwell passed me on the way in and told me the situation. His son suffers from low blood sugar; if he does not get his regular medicine, he won't stay healthy long enough for whatever they have planned. He asked me, as a favor, to request permission to send them a message and ask if they have the medicine for that. If not, Commander Jere's doctor can give him the medicine required," he explained.

In response, the General turned to the signalman, "Trooper, you get that?"

"Yes sir," the trooper replied. General Chester nodded and the message was sent. A few moments later, they received a reply.

"Sir, they say they have the medicine and advise us he is getting the full Dark Empire hospitality treatment," the trooper translating the flashes finished reporting.

"There you go, Admiral William, you can inform Jere's dad, and please advise him that is the last favor he gets. Next, gather all senior officers to join me in the briefing room straight away. Also, summon the White Knight representatives again," he ordered. William instantly saluted, soon as the sentence left the General's mouth, and left to carry out the orders.

"Sir?" Commander Douglas asked as they started to walk back. "Permission to speak freely, sir?"

General Chester nodded.

"Sir, forgive me. This is not me doubting your abilities to lead us, sir, however, we need Commander Rockwell in charge to be able keep them in check. If they learn he is not in charge, we will lose every advantage we have and lose the appearance that we are strong. If all they have to do is capture our family members to break us, they will forever keep using that tactic against us.

Also, only Rockwell can set off the charges, regardless if you are in command or not…"

"Get to the point, Commander," the General said with his stern voice, interrupting Douglas mid-way.

"Right, sir. Thing is, I know as well as you, the policy states that one man is expendable and we have to assume Jere is already dead and not to risk anything to get him back. However, the policy was not written for this situation. We need Rockwell in command and fully alert, not with mixed emotions of a father; we need the General. We are going to have to go with whatever they have planned or do what we can to secure Commander Jere back. If they kill him or we lose him, we lose this planet. He will not be in a state to do his duty, and Coroscate made it clear no one else has the authority, not even you. Their reason, sir, was to prevent a power struggle and put down any ideas of mutiny. So with that much said, it is pretty clear what you must do." Douglas finished speaking as he put his pipe back in his mouth to continue smoking on the way up.

"Thank you, Commander. Well, we have an hour and I want to let everyone know what is going on. I will make a decision at the end of the meeting," General Chester said as they both walked away.

~

"Apprentice, you are sure about this? You are taking a very big risk," Biaci remarked.

"Look who is talking, you the master of risk taking," Fortis replied with

41

a smile. "Yes, I know the risk, but it is a calculated risk. They will need Commander Jere back. I know his dad well enough. He loves his son and right now, I suspect he is falling apart right about now," she finished saying.

"What is it, Captain David?" Biaci turned to see the captain approaching from the barricade.

"Enemy signaled us, my lord. They informed us the prisoner suffers from low blood sugar; we will need to administer the medicine for that illness to him if we want him alive to be able to trade him." Captain David stood to attention.

"I'll do it, Master; I used to do it for him all the time." Fortis replied, looking at her master. "Is he still unconscious?" Biaci nodded, and with that, Fortis, still on crutches, hopped away to see the doctor, leaving Captain David with Biaci.

"Captain, I want you to escort Fortis when we escort our wounded. Do you have the work party ready for when they agree?" she asked.

"My Lady, nothing will happen. The work detail is ready. Are you worried about your apprentice, or worried she may be turned back?" he questioned with a serious look.

"Her past died when I saw her torture the prisoner; she has no love for the Republic. I just feel she is getting in over herself," Biaci replied.

"Here is the remote you asked me to construct. It is programmed to send a signal over the frequency you told me to set it to. You still not going to tell me what it is for?" Captain David asked as he handed over the remote.

"What is the maximum range?" Biaci demanded.

"I would say, any ships sitting in orbit would pick it up, but no further than that," the Captain replied. "My Lord, you can trust me; I am loyal to the Emperor. Whatever it is you have planned, I'll understand."

"I don't think you will. My main concern is my standing orders, given to make sure the Republic doesn't know the Dark Knights are still alive…"

Biaci was interrupted as a large ship flew in over their heads towards the Headquarters building.

"That's a White Knight Shuttle!" Biaci shouted. She ran up to the Barricade. "Dammit, which is the tallest building we have?" Captain David pointed in response.

Nothing else needed saying. Biaci ran at top speed, using the Dark power to blast open doors in her way as she ran upstairs with her incredible speed. She reached the top of the roof, and could see the Republic spotters all around them, now focusing on her.

She walked up to the edge, level with the Barricade. Using the glasses found in the tanks, she looked through directly at the new shuttle as its occupants were disembarking following the its arrival. Finally Captain David arrived, out of breath, hunched over with his hands on his knees.

"What...Phew!...What is it, my Lady?" he asked, trying to catch his breath as he spoke.

"WHITE KNIGHT, DAMMIT!!!" Biaci screamed out and she crushed the glasses in her hand from her anger. She looked out over the roofs, seeing all the spotters and their partners with their guns aimed directly at her.

"I've HAD IT with the Republic scum!" She stood still in the middle of the roof, hands out at her side. She closed her fists as she tilted her head and closed her eyes. She remembered the pain and hurt of her brother's betrayal, the pain of being used as her master's weapon, the emotional pain of killing her brother, the enjoyment of killing him, the anger of seeing her home, the feelings as she killed the Republic soldier who wanted to rape her.

She remembered the anger she felt seeing that man shoot Danielle, her apprentice. It welled up inside of her, in sync with the power radiating inside her body. Both arms shot up into the air, and all the Republic sharp shooter teams followed suit, quickly rising into the air. They floated there, dangling from the sky. Everyone put their hands over their chests and started moaning, as pain began spreading throughout their bodies.

Captain David stood there in awe, unable to do anything but watch. The weapons fell off the roofs into the Non-Republic district. He would have someone collect all the useful weapons, but at the moment he was still frozen watching this Dark Knight in all her anger.

Suddenly it was all over as all of the Republic sharp shooter teams were killed by having their hearts ripped out of their chests. Biaci turned around, still in a trance, to face the Republic lines. Both arms were now straight pointing directly ahead as all the bodies flew towards the Republic lines like Ragdolls.

"Captain…" Biaci began, not sounding like herself at all. "You will need to obtain a long range transmitter or a holo communicator when you escort them. Our friends must be close." She looked up at him now. " They have prisoners, Dark Military prisoners. They must have been the advance scouts, which means my master and the Emperor will not be far behind." Still enraged with her power, Biaci tried to calm herself down as she walked off to go see her Apprentice. She knew the plan had changed.

~

The White Knight shuttle from the super dreadnaught landed, met by a small Republic security force. General Chester came out to greet Master Sergio, who saluted the General as he disembarked.

"I have something for you to send back to Coroscate that should get you your reinforcements that you need. My ship will start to resupply; you have your quartermasters send their lists," he said in an expressionless voice.

"Master Sergio," General Chester said as he grabbed the White Knight's hand to shake. "You don't know how glad we are to see you. Your timely arrival will be a great help to us…" General Chester trailed off as he noticed the Prisoners being led off now.

"I was informed you intend to send the Centaur back to get the attention of the government; I think this should be a very clear message that you intend to send. Unfortunately, my communications was destroyed, so I have no means of long range communications or relaying the signal from here back to Coroscate as was done before. However, we have secured you a nice clear message. Now update me on the details please. Where is General Rockwell?" he asked with a puzzled look, looking around as if expecting the General to appear.

"He relieved himself of command until negotiations have been completed. The enemy has the General's son, Commander Jere. We wanted to offer a ceasefire. However, with commander Jere in their hands, they have modified the terms, which to be fair, they are not unreasonable terms."

He turned around to look at the prisoners.

"We need to get them back soon as possible," Chester decided then and there. He walked over to the trooper who had escorted him up to the shuttle. "Signal the  enemy. Tell them the deal is accepted; ceasefire for forty eight hours, starts in twenty minutes after their response."

"SIR!" one of the guards shouted. They all looked up to see the bodies of their men crashing to the floor in the middle of the lines.

It was Master Sergio who responded, "It is okay, General. We made the Dark Knight angry. They must have seen the prisoners, as I hoped they would."

"Proceed with the ceasefire offer," General Chester ordered.

~

Fortis arrived in the room and left the door open as she entered. The two guards remained alert as they stayed outside by the door. She saw the unconscious body of Commander Jere lying on the table.

"Commander?" She shook his shoulder to make sure he was not just sleeping. No response. She checked for a pulse by placing her index finger and middle finger on the side of the Commander's throat. She was relieved to feel the steady pulse.

"Good. Your dad always did love you. Despite all his faults, his one redeeming quality is his love for you. Even now, he is looking out for you." She rolled up the sleeve on his right arm past his shoulder and placed the needle to push the contents into his system.

"Why? Danielle, we loved each other," Commander Jere said slowly.

This surprised Fortis, but her surprise passed as quickly as it came.

"Because I've sat outside your dad's office for too long, and seen what kind of person he is, the kind of person you are. You are your father's son, you always were. You don't see anything wrong with what he has done here, do you?" She looked at him seriously.

"He has made you angry is what I see he has done wrong. Driving you away brings me closer to you, not him," he responded.

"Quite, and that narrow vision is why you are like your dad. You don't see what he did to these people is horrible. I loved you once, but not anymore." She looked at him directly in his eyes. "It's over Jere. I don't love you, I can't love you."

Fortis suddenly looked towards the door and saw her master standing there

She stood up instantly. "Master!" she exclaimed as she bowed her head.

"The plan has changed slightly they have prisoners from the Dark military…" Biaci started to say.

"My lord, my lord!" someone shouted from behind Biaci. She turned to see Captain David running towards her. "They've accepted; we have ten minutes now to get ready. They've sent a request we allow their doctor to come inspect Commander Jere. Also, to see the person who needs surgery. He is waiting to come over now." He paused to wait for an answer.

"Send the acknowledgment. Give permission for their doctor. He is to be unharmed, but watched the entire time," Biaci ordered. "Apprentice, walk with me."

Captain David went off to send the reply as Fortis joined her master. Both Master and Apprentice started to head towards the barricade.

"So, we will have you escorted, as you know. Captain David will escort you and stay with you until your return. However, the plan needs to be altered. David has instructions to get a transmitter of any kind, so you are going to have be left unguarded for a while. I want you to have this on you." Biaci handed her a small white capsule.

"It is your last resort; they will be hard on you, if they can. You have made them angry and if their doctor reports to them what his condition is, they will know you helped us with him. So, if you get into a situation take that and bite into it, and you will fall asleep before anything can happen to you."

Biaci paused looking at her apprentice as the Republic doctor arrived.

"Ah, greetings, Doctor." The doctor was a short man, just five foot, four inches tall, wearing spectacles, and an old fashioned stethoscope. He stopped short of Biaci and bowed his head. Then he turned to see Fortis.

"Daughter," he said quietly with a half-smile.

Biaci looked seriously at her apprentice. "So that is why you were so skillful with our doctor," she said with a smile. Fortis went over to her dad and gave him a hug.

"I take it you are the patient requesting surgery?" He knelt down and looked at the stub of where Fortis' right foot had once been. "Who cleaned you up? They didn't do a bad job except..." He adjusted the bandage and pulled some antiseptic out of his bag, placing it on her wound. Suddenly the Rear guard doctor came running up.

"What is going here? What are you doing to my patient?" he demanded. Fortis' dad looked up at him.

"Come see for yourself," he said with a smile as the Rear guard doctor knelt down.

"Oh, I see. You've stopped the infection from being able to come back. Clever." He stood up. "I'm Doctor Hassan." The Rear Guard doctor put his hand out to shake the Republic doctor's hand.

"I'm Doctor Slowcombe, your patient's father," he said as they shook hands.

"That explains it. She helped me out during a complicated procedure. She made a great nurse, directing where incisions had to be made. It was a pleasure to work with someone that was not blood shy." Fortis' dad smiled at her with a proud-father type smile. Dr. Hassan pointed the way to where Commander Jere was. He had started to walk over with Dr. Slowcombe, but stopped when he saw Slowcombe had gone over to his daughter.

"You know what you are doing?" he asked of her.

"Yes, Father, I do. My master, Biaci, has been great; she has looked after me and been very kind. We are doing the right thing." She looked down at her foot.

"Commander Powell did it," she said with a sad look. Dr. Slowcombe turned to Biaci.

"I am grateful to you for looking after her. You welcomed the cook staff from Rockwell's kitchen staff. Would you extend the same offer to my medical team? There is a number of other staff too that were from the other cities that was forced to line up with them. We have no argument against you. Seeing my daughter, hearing what she has to say, is all I need. If she says this is the right thing to do, then I am helping the wrong side."

"The offer is extended. If they want to come over, either to join us or to just sit out the conflict during the ceasefire, they will be welcomed. Your son, Fortis' brother, is at the storage barn, if you have time to see him." Biaci stated, nodding her head.

"Apprentice, we need you at the barricade," she said as she began to walk away. Fortis hugged her dad once more, and Dr. Slowcombe went off with Dr. Hassan to inspect Commander Jere.

~

"Time is up; send out the work party," Commander Douglas ordered. The eight Republic men went out with stretchers and medical packs. Six medical droids followed them out to the no man's land. They left their supplies in the center, and set out to collect their dead and wounded. The work detail from the Non-Republic district came to collect the supplies. As the sounds of water started to come on throughout the district, people rushed to take showers and get clean, brushing their teeth and washing their clothes.

The Republic signalman sent a series of flashes, and quickly received a reply.

"They are coming now, sir," he reported to Commander Douglas.

"Tell the Centaur to stand-by." Douglas responded as he started to look through his glasses. "Open up the lines; they are NOT to be harmed," he shouted as he watched the parade of wounded, all dressed in Dark Military uniforms, wearing their patches on their shoulders with pride. At the head of the parade was the Republic Doctor, Dr. Slowcombe, with a patient on a stretcher. Douglas looked through his glasses.

"Oh, make sure there is a strong guard on the Centaur; they must not be harmed. Commander Jere's life depends on it. Place Captain Powell under arrest," Douglas ordered. A foot soldier went off to carry out the order.

As the parade approached, the doctor saluted to the Commander.

"Sir, I have personally seen Commander Jere. His condition is fair. He is talking; they have treated him well." He didn't stop walking as he spoke and carried on towards the ship.

Back in the Headquarters building, both Generals Chester and Rockwell were looking out the window, watching the parade.

"Last time we were standing here, our roles were reversed. Now, I am standing here and I can appreciate everything you did. I'm sorry if I ever judge you too harshly." Chester offered his hand, and Rockwell accepted.

"Thank you for doing this it can't be easy." Rockwell stated.

"Sir, please don't get me wrong, but your son is not why I accepted. We need to get that ship back to Coroscate soon as possible; the longer we delay, the bigger the risk something will happen. It means they have help coming if we were able to catch prisoners this far out. Now, we have no long range communications. We have to get the Centaur back, so we get the reinforcements." He looked at Rockwell. "You have any more of that brandy?" Rockwell smiled as he walked over to get the bottle and drinking glasses.

"Right now, we still hold the advantage," Rockwell started to say when a knock sounded on the door. "Enter," Rockwell commanded, and a trooper entered.

"Sir, Douglas compliments the doctor, reports he has seen Commander Jere and he is talking. Commander Douglas has placed Captain Powell under arrest for the duration of the ceasefire. The person needing surgery is your former clerk; her name now, reportedly, is Fortis. She has become an apprentice to the Dark Knight Master, Biaci."

"Where are they now?" Rockwell demanded, putting down his glass.

"She is being prepped for surgery. Her father, and her escort, a Captain David, is with them."

Rockwell stormed out the door, leaving Chester behind. "You've done it now, trooper," Chester said as he ran after Rockwell.

On board the ship's surgical room, the medical staff orderlies placed Fortis on the table. Captain David stood by the door in a surgical gown with a mask on, not taking his eyes off Fortis. The doctor looked over the foot again, one more time.

"It will not be hard; I've already selected a good replacement for you." He looked towards his daughter and she tried to smile, but it was obvious anxiety was starting to show.

"It will be okay," he said as he squeezed her hand.

"I'm sorry, Dad," she said to him. "I'm sorry if I made you worry."

"Nonsense. You've made me very proud. It doesn't matter what color uniform you wear; I am still your dad and you are my daughter. I will always love you. You followed your heart and I couldn't be more proud. Now rest." He turned around to start getting prepared.

"Your dad is a good man, Fortis," Captain David remarked. Just then, the doors opened and Rockwell stormed in.

"Why?! Why did you do it?" Rockwell demanded. Captain David stepped forward. "Relax, I won't harm her. I want my son, after all," he said toward David. "Your fiancée. You were like my own daughter.

Why did you betray me? ...betray us?" he questioned, directing his attention back to Fortis.

Fortis propped herself up on her elbows to better talk to him and pointed towards her right leg, "Because this is your handiwork; you didn't pull the trigger, however, you might as well have. You force people to do what you want them to do, or you make them suffer for it. That is no choice at all. You actually sent in the tanks to slaughter all them people and all they did was steal your food because you starved them. Why?

"Because they didn't want to play with you. You are just a typical pompous bully that thinks everyone wants and should play with you, and if they don't, you punish them for it. Except these people will not lay down, they fight before they die.

"Whatever the Dark Empire did, or the Dark Knights did, beforehand does not make what you are doing to them now right: they were civilians," she finished saying.

"Please General, we need to get started and you are increasing her heart rate. No harm must come to her, remember that." The doctor put a firm hand on the General's shoulder and started to force him out. "You too, Captain; you can guard the door."

Pausing at the door for a moment, the general said, "He loved you, you know." With that, he was gone. The door shut behind the doctor as he saw Rockwell and David out. Fortis laid back down and tried to relax. Then suddenly, the lights went out.

"Dad?" Fortis cried out. She heard something being slid through the door handles, barring the door from opening. Again, she tried calling out, "Dad, what is going on?"

"I wanted to chat with you one-on-one for a moment," a voice said slowly. "I'm sorry for your injury and any suffering you went through. I was aiming for something higher. However, you got lucky."

"Powell!" she exclaimed. He slowly started to walk up to her, "You know we gave you everything; you had all you possibly could want. You even... letting you take Rockwell's son to bed, when we all knew you were loose." He placed his left hand on her left leg and started rubbing the inside of her leg, gradually moving his hand upward.

Fortis attempted to slap his arm away, but he stopped her with his right hand. "You've switched sides; you've joined the rejects, so the laws that protected you no longer apply to you. I do not care if Jere lives or not; I'm leaving with the ship." His left hand reached up and now was rubbing her inner thigh. "Because of you, they reduced me to the rank of Captain."

"Perhaps you should learn to shoot better," she retorted as she tried to fight him off. This made Powell lash her hands to the table above her head.

"Trust me, I never miss." He put a rag from the side table inside her mouth. Her dad and Captain David began shouting and loudly banging on the door.

"I guess I have to skip the foreplay." He tore apart the gown Fortis was wearing, revealing Fortis' body. "So plain... I fail to see what Jere saw in you. I can see he over exaggerated the details." He climbed on top of Fortis and leaned over, kissing the side of her neck as tears started to flow from her eyes. Powell's hands wrapped around her breasts as she felt his erection. She kept looking away and heard him unzip his pants. He started to grunt as she felt him going inside her.

She closed her eyes, trying to get through it alive. After what seemed like forever, Powell collapsed on top of her. She opened her eyes and saw everyone in the room, General Rockwell, her dad, Captain David, and a large compliment of Republic guards.

"It's over now," Captain David said as he untied her hands and removed her gag. She was frozen. General Rockwell didn't say a word. Apparently, as angry as he was for her choices, he didn't want to see her like this. He retrieved a rescue blanket and handed it to Captain David, who placed it over Fortis.

"Do the surgery now, Dad. No sedation," she demanded.

"But..." her dad protested.

"No sedation. I survived having my foot taken off; I am sure I can survive this. I want Captain David with me." She watched them take Powell away.

"General…?" she was about to ask.

"You've joined the Dark Empire. There is nothing that can be done; he did not break any Republic laws." He looked directly at her.

"Even though he committed the crime on Republic ground?" she asked.

"Rest now, you going to have a tough time now." He left the room.

Fortis looked at Captain David and said, "You are going to wish you had Biaci's skill of not feeling pain."

"I'm here for you, Fortis," he said as his arms wrapped around her. He held of both her hands tight as the procedure began.

"I'll try to be quick, Danielle," Dr. Slowcombe said.

"Don't be quick, do it well, Dad, like an expert doctor," Fortis pleaded. She started to feel the pain welling up inside her. She closed her eyes as if trying to force out the pain, still upset and angry with what had happened, with being raped. She thought of Biaci, her master, and somehow she was able to start seeing her with her mind's eye. "I'm sorry, Master. I couldn't stop him; he hurt me," Fortis said, not knowing if she was just saying it to herself or not.

"What is wrong Fortis? I sense you from here; why are you not sedated?" Biaci responded.

"Powell raped me, Master. There was nothing I could do. I insisted they do the surgery without sedation. Captain David is with me now. They are not going to punish him. I want to make the offer they send Powell to you in exchange for Jere. They won't kill him; I want him dead."

"Do you know what you are saying?" Biaci quizzed Fortis.

"Yes, it means they could keep me. We won't have any leverage. I want him dead." Fortis repressed a scream as she could not hold back the tears anymore.

"Master, please?" Fortis pleaded.

"Explain it to Captain David. If he agrees, okay," Biaci ordered.

Fortis opened her eyes and saw David wiping her forehead. "I want to trade the prisoner for Powell; I want him dead. My master said to ask you what you think."

"How are you not screaming in agony?" he questioned. She tugged his hand.

"What do you …er …think?" she repeated.

"Does it mean that much to you?" David asked as he stood up while looking at her directly, still holding her hand tight as she started to draw blood from his hand. "You willing to give up your freedom for revenge?"

"Have you ever been raped, Captain? I wanted to kill him before for losing my leg, but this is something else. No woman can rest knowing the person who violated them is walking around freely. You never forget a single detail," she finished, just looking at David as tears came flooding from her eyes.

"Doctor, I just have to say, you have an amazing daughter, a wonderful woman." Dr. Slowcombe looked towards him. "I'll go speak to the General. I need to do my assigned task anyway too," he said to Fortis with a wink.

One of the nurses took Captain David's place as he ran out, leaving Fortis. Captain David ran to the offices where he knew the General would be, but was stopped by the guards.

"Can we help you, sir?" they asked of him.
"I have a message for General Rockwell from my General concerning his son," he replied.

One of the guards briefly looked at the other before going into the office. Shortly after, the doors were opened and the guard ushered Captain David inside the office.

Captain David marched in, stood to attention and saluted. Rockwell, accompanied by General Chester, looked but didn't return the salute.

"Thank you for seeing me, Generals," David started to say.

"We extend our sympathy for what happened to Danielle; it is regrettable. He was under arrest and will be court marshaled, however, we cannot prosecute him for hurting Danielle. She is outside the law now," Rockwell announced.

"Indeed. I have been authorized to offer an adjustment to the deal. We are willing to exchange your officer for your son. This has been considered by all parties and Fortis knows what she is doing by offering this exchange." He gave General Rockwell a serious look.

However, it was Chester who responded, "Captain, you are saying you are willing to exchange officers, giving away your leverage? Danielle will be held as a prisoner of war. You are sure about this?"

"We are, sir. If I may be permitted to have a short transmitter or holo communicator, I can go back to Fortis and communicate with my General that you agree to arrange the deal?" David asked.

The two generals turned around and walked away from the Captain, so he could not see or overhear what was said a few moments later. They approached again after a few moments.

"Very well, the deal is accepted. We will exchange Captain Powell for Commander Jere in thirty minutes. The guard will give you a transmitter."

~

"My Lord, the Republic work parties have come to collect the prisoner. Also, those wishing to defect have come over," Captain Jack reported to Biaci.

"Are they ready to make the exchange?" she asked.

"Come look. Captain David is next to the man in chains. Your apprentice is standing next to their General, my Lord." The captain left to rejoin the barricade.

Biaci headed back up on top of their tallest building to look. She could see her apprentice standing on crutches, not looking happy at all, with her dad to her left and General Rockwell to her right.

"Start the exchange!" Biaci shouted and it started. The Republic work party began to walk slowly with Commander Jere on the stretcher, while the Non-Republic work detail, who had escorted the wounded to the ship, started to move with Captain David and Powell in custody. He looked back towards Fortis with a sort of half smile.

They had reached about half way when General Rockwell, from behind, pushed Fortis forward. "Go, you are brave. I'm sorry for what happened to you. I owe you for looking after my son while in your care. Now, do me a favor, make sure you make it hurt." He placed a short knife in her hand. Astonished, she looked up at the General.

"Thank you, sir." She turned and walked off, followed by her dad. Then she started to run. Biaci watched intensely as she could feel the anger storming inside her apprentice.

Fortis came charging up behind Powell while David still had hold of him. She tackled Powell to the ground, knocking him loose from David, and stabbed him in his right arm.

"LEAVE US," she shouted.

Everyone proceeded onward; Jere was safely back and the Dark Empire forces were back behind the barricade. It was just Powell and Fortis left in the middle of the no man's land.

"This is from General Rockwell; he said to make it painful," she said as she slowly sliced into his chest and cut down towards his stomach. It wasn't quite deep enough to make him start bleeding.

She removed his chains and restraints, and waited for him to get back up. As soon as he did, she swung for him with her right fist and landed it to the sound of a tremendous cheer from behind the barricade.

She went to kick him to the ground, but he came back at her, picked her up by the waist, and dropped her into the mud on the ground. This time the Republic soldiers cheered, except for General Rockwell.

"Looks like you want some more fun, whore," he said as he let the blood drop on to her face. She kneed him hard in the groin and he rolled over in pain. Men from both forces could be heard moaning "oooh..." while some of the them not even in the fight went to cover their groins as if feeling the pain that Powell had to be feeling now.

"What is the matter? Don't like it when we girls fight back? Oh wait, I already know you are not a man; you are a coward. You wait and make it, so we cannot fight back." She punched him again, this time drawing blood, and he spat it out in Fortis' face.

"Come on, Fortis. Kill him," Biaci said to herself quietly. She saw Fortis kick him in the face and then stomp on each elbow, breaking the joints.

"Now, we have some time," Fortis said with a vindictive tone. "This is how you like it, right? Unable to fight back? Helpless?" She pulled off his pants. "The General did say make it painful, so..." She knelt down and sliced off his penis. Powell screamed in agony while the Republic soldiers were silent now. Fortis rolled him onto his side and inserted what remained of his penis into Powell's anus. "Hey, look at that, now you can actually fuck yourself."

She fell onto his chest, and sitting astride him, she made the already cut chest bleed out more. She moved her hands over his chest, bathing her hands in his blood. Then she leaned forward and grasped her hands around his throat.

"You made the biggest mistake by letting me live," she sneered as she started to squeeze. Captain Powell, unable to speak, opened his mouth to try to breathe. Fortis inserted the capsule Biaci had given her and forced him to bite down on the cap, breaking it. "It is a quicker death than you deserve."

She looked down at the dead Captain Powell, then over to the Republic lines, and took two steps forward.

"You see this pile of shit on the ground? He raped me. I swear it, White Knight. Dammit, I swear it. Any one of you come at me or my friends, I will do the same to you as I did to him.

"The Emperor will set foot on Rriban again. Go now and live; stay and we will kill you."

She turned and went to join her cheering comrades. Biaci was lost for words; she knew she had the apprentice she wanted. She pulled out the remote, checked it still had signal, and placed it back in her pocket.

As soon as Commander Jere reached their lines, Rockwell was at his side and escorted him, on his stretcher, to the Centaur hospital ship, now full with Dark military prisoners, their own wounded, and wounded people of the city. It was time for the ship to launch.

Rockwell assumed command as General again, now that the negotiations were over. General Chester was all too happy to be back as acting commander again. The ship took off. It was painted white with a huge medical symbol, and the words "hospital ship" were painted in every known language.

The ship just got off the ground as Commander Jere was placed on one of the hospital beds and hooked up to an IV drip. Just below Commander Jere were the ship's fuel tanks; they provided extra heat when the ship was moving, which was a great comfort to the patients on board.

The Centaur had just broken into orbit. Biaci had the remote in her hand, and at the same time in space, another Dark Empire scout ship came out of stealth and fired its missiles. The two missiles hit at the exact same time as Biaci's thumb hit the button; the remote set off the detonator in Jere's shoulder, which ruptured the fuel tanks.

# Part 2

# CHAPTER 9

"Report. Is there any survivors?" Sweeper demanded.

"Apologies, ma'am, we have no functioning commands; we are only able to see what they transmit. They managed to relay a signal to the pod they were able to launch, however, the scout ship crew stopped responding," reported Reader Eight.

Everyone was looking at their screens, all looking at the same image, they saw the hospital ship exploding. However, because the ship was still in orbit of the planet and in the planet's gravity, it did not blow up into particle dust, which would have been kinder. As there were small amounts of oxygen left, it allowed the fire to breathe. Right then, they could see people scrambling to escape pods, while large amounts of women were burning alive.

"LOOK! There is Dark Military prisoners on there too, White Knight. Damn it, poor bastards," Reader Four reported.

"Get me in contact with that scout ship that fired. Use the pod to relay communications to it," ordered Sweeper.

"I am not positive we can get it to work..." a Fixer reported.

"Get it working! I don't care how," Sweeper demanded, interrupting the Fixer. "Captain Tyrik, use that screen over there. Report to the Emperor, please, then get me through to the Emperor's Saber. The Dark Council has orders not to disturb the Saber, but it is imperative I get through to her."

She didn't wait for a response to turn back around. Sweeper was in her element now, while Cryptic M's talent was keeping a stiff upper lip. This Sweeper talent was to be able to stay organized and collected in a crisis.

"Sweeper, the Fixer did it. Communication open with that scout ship; audio only, the signal is weak, however," Reader Eight reported.

Sweeper didn't hesitate. She walked over to the console and stated, "Captain, this is Sweeper at Intelligence. Do you receive me?"

"Yes, Sweeper. This is Captain Jarad of Scout Ship 016. I know what you are going to ask, that explosion was not the result of us. There had to be a detonation from inside at the same time," the Captain reported.

"What is the status of your ship?" she asked.

"Hundred percent fully operational," he reported.

"Captain Jarad, I am giving you a direct order to land and help the Rear Guard. Make sure your radio is intact and put whoever is in charge in front of that radio; we need to know what is going on. They will need your ship's defenses to defend against the Republic, I am sure of it. Sweeper out." Sweeper turned off the connection.

"Captain Tyrik, you get permission to speak to the Saber?" She turned on him next.

"Yes, Sweeper," he said quietly. Sweeper went to the conference hall and proceeded to her office.

"By order of the Emperor, you are hereby in temporary command of Intelligence." Captain Tyrik whispered to Reader Eight. The Reader looked at him with a stunned expression.

Tyrik performed a circle gesture with his hands and all the guards formed up on him. He then proceeded to head towards Sweeper's office.

Tyrik proceeded into the office to see Sweeper starting to get frustrated while trying to turn on her display.

"It's not working. I am entering my commands, but it's not responding," she stated as she tapped the display.

"Ma'am," Tyrik said.

"I'm busy, Captain. I have to speak to the Saber; it is important."

"Ma'am!" he repeated more insistently. That did the trick, as she looked up and saw he had all his guards with him.

"What is the problem, Captain?" she asked with an honest look. Captain Tyrik simply pointed and the four guards stood around her.

"Ma'am, I'm sorry, Emperor's orders. You are hereby under arrest, pending an investigation and the judgement from the Emperor," he said with a sad look.

"What!? Why?!" she asked, astonished.

"The Saber reported to the Emperor, the enemy General on Rriban received a transmission from someone on Kaas. Intelligence is the only building with the capability of long range communications. Again, the only person who can do such a thing is Sweeper. Therefore until cleared, you are under arrest. Please do not make this harder than it already is," he finished with a nod. The two guards behind her put a hand under each arm and escorted her down to the cells.

Captain Tyrik went to the display in the wall to make the priority call, entering his Guard code and the extra security given by the Emperor. The screen turned on and Duplex Agens' face appeared.

"My Lord," he said, doing a half bow.

"Captain? Not that this isn't a nice surprise, however, why are you using Sweeper's terminal?" Duplex had a puzzled look on her face.

"Emperor has placed her under arrest. Someone is trying to frame her; I know she is innocent." He looked down, then back up. "However, that is not why I contacted you. Did you see the explosion of that hospital ship?" he asked and she nodded in confirmation.

"The scout ship responsible was ordered to land, and provide assistance, and put their radio in front of your apprentice. Emperor's order, you must not delay you have to get to Rriban within the next two days." He finished with his orders that he had been given, "Reader Eight is acting Sweeper now."

"Captain," Duplex interrupted.

"Yes, ma'am," he responded.

"Tell me the truth; I can easily use the Dark power to get the truth out from you. If Sweeper is your friend, you need to tell me what you know. If it is not her that is the traitor, then someone else more dangerous is," she responded. "I order you to tell me the truth," she added. "There, now you do not have to feel bad about betraying anyone's trust. You were ordered and as a guard you have to obey."

"My Lord, the day Lord Thant entered into here and Sweeper was missing, she was with me and Dark Knight Killtooth," he replied.

"What would you three be doing together? … Oh," realization hit Duplex as she asked. "I understand now, Captain. Way to go, Sweeper. Never knew she had it in her," she said, trying to calm the Captain down.

"Neither did I, my Lord. She was in a real state. I found her outside headquarters very upset, uncontrollable really. I took her to the tavern here in Kaas City in the officers section. That is where Killtooth met up with us. She relaxed after a couple of drinks and we went back to mine and Killtooth's place, and you can guess what happened. However, there is a whole tavern that can provide her an alibi," he stated.

"What was she upset about?" Duplex questioned.

"She was not permitted to say; it was the day you left Kaas. All she said was 'Cryptic M was the lucky one; he got a statue,'" he recited.

"Oh, I see, I guess she was a lot closer to Fidus than I realized. Captain, relax. What you do with your love life is your own concern. I am glad you informed me. Who else knows of this?" she asked.

"No one, my Lady. Your apprentice, Fidus, he is dead?" he asked.

"He got sent away on a mission, a very dangerous mission, Captain," she lied. "So no one heard her say this to you? Good, keep it that way. Although unfortunate, it may keep her safe. Whoever is trying to frame her may move about more confidently, more likely to make a mistake. I'll let the Emperor know. It was nice to see you again, Captain." With that, the screen went black.

There was a knock on the door as the Captain took a minute to pause and collect himself again. He turned to see Reader Eight standing there.

"I apologize, I didn't mean to intrude," said Reader Eight, now acting

Sweeper.

"I always believed she was party girl under that hard exterior." She gave a nervous laugh.

The Captain couldn't help but to chuckle with her. "My apologies, this is your office now. The same guard detail will apply to you." He stood to attention as she walked into the office.

"I know she is innocent. She went through hell to gain the trust of Cryptic M. She loved him." Reader Eight walked over and sat down. As soon as she did the automated voice came on throughout the building, "Transfer of power completed. Former designation Reader Eight, now present Sweeper."

# CHAPTER 10

"How long before the engines are repaired?" Sarah questioned.

"I can fix it faster if people stop asking me that," said a muffled voice. The man was knee-deep in cables and turbine engine parts with bolts and screws laying around.

"So, do you know what the problem even is?" Sarah then asked.

"Yeah, the White Knight Scum fired their fucking weapons at us, disabling the Engines." The man sighed, still not looking up.

"Considering the Morgan Rice is having the same problem, you thought about contacting the Engineer over there to cut the work load in half?" she asked, already knowing the answer.

"Why would I do that?" he replied, voice still muffled.

"I don't know, because perhaps the White Knight scum fired their fucking weapons at their engines, disabling them too?" She'd heard enough. She walked over to clothes rack holding spare engineer uniforms; she grabbed one and put it on over her uniform.

This of all things made the Engineer look up. Then he noticed the uniform, arm patch included. He tried wiping the dirt and grease from his eyes with his hand, but it only made it worse. He looked down, realizing his hands were covered in just as much grease. He picked up a rag he had laying aside, wiped his face, and looked again. She was looking back at him now.

"What do they call you?" she demanded.

"Morecambe, ma'am," he saluted. "Apologies, I didn't know," he said with a very apologetic voice.

"Hmm, well, what have you checked so far?" She looked around. There were signs of his handy work, with parts of machines and engines laying around everywhere.

"I've checked it all; they are all working. I've replaced the parts that got fried from the blasts; they just will not work. This was the last place to look," he shrugged.

"So, you are now guessing." She picked up a flash light that was on a head band and jumped down, Morecambe had open the floor crates to access the electronic features to the engines. She laid on her back and slid under the opposite section from where he was.

"You just going to stand there?" she asked.

This made him jump and he got back down. Nobody said a word as they continued to examine the electronics section.

"Morecambe, were you here during the combat?" she inquired.

"I was in the control room doing damage control. That is my battle station," he replied.

"You know what you have discovered by saying what you did earlier?" she was slightly muffled now as she went in deeper.

"I said I replaced the parts that was damaged and it still doesn't work." He tried to remember or think of what that could imply.

"How do machines break?" she tried to walk him through this, as if talking to a toddler.

"By neglect or interactions with people," he replied, still not getting the hint.

"Did you neglect to do your duty aboard this ship?" she asked, seeing if this would get him the hint needed.

"No, I'm always alert. These engines are like my children," he said. "Wait a minute…" Hearing that, Sarah smiled to herself.

"If the blasts from the White Knights only damaged the parts I replaced, having replaced the broken parts and the engines still don't work, that means some other person interfered with the engines." Suddenly alert, he tried to sit up with the realization and smacked his head on the machine parts. "Ouch!" he exclaimed, and Sarah laughed.

"Get out of there, we need to check something," Morecambe ordered. Then remembering who he was talking to, he added, "Ma'am."

With a sense of urgency, he got out of the floor, ran over to a control panel, and started working on it. Sarah was wiping her hands on a rag as she came up behind him.

"Unless things have changed in the eight years I was gone, the only way is by remote or manually, meaning someone on the ship would be a traitor. However, they would have to be on both ships at the same time, so look for a remote signal. That is more likely," she said.

"Right." He looked over his left shoulder, then turned back. "Ma'am, beg your pardon for saying so, but you look pretty with grease all over you." The sound of buttons being pushed disguised his nervousness.

"You don't see many women?" she asked of him.

"Plenty, but none that would jump into an engine suit and risk getting grease in their hair. Plenty of office clerks, even some on the front lines. None that want to get dirty." He looked down. "Okay... yes, I checked the logs. A remote signal was received at the same time that the blasts hit the ship. They been remotely deactivated and locked down. They will not work until the lock is lifted."

Sarah, hearing that, walked over to the side monitor and pushed it. "Computer, initiate secure call: Emperor's Saber." The screen displayed the word "Connecting..."

"Yes, Sarah?" Duplex inquired.

"You need to come down here. We've discovered something. Bring the Admiral," Sarah stated.

"Does it have anything to do with why you are covered in grease?"

Sarah didn't get to reply, Morecambe spoke, "Captain, I found something else."

"I am on my way," Duplex said, ending the call.

Morecambe continued, "I traced the signal, only the Emperor can personally shut down the ships remotely. Besides him, the Dark Intelligence can shut down a ship in case of mutiny, and well, look."

Sarah leaned over and saw the display, "Sweeper code Zulu, transmit shut down received 14:00."

Morecambe locked the screen to make sure no one else could see until Duplex arrived with the Admiral.

He turned around. "So, perhaps we could get something to eat sometime? … When you are not busy, of course."

"I would like that. I am going to be busy for a while, so after we are done here, we can just skip the food and go straight to your room, if you prefer?" She winked. "I've been on Rriban for eight years. Not exactly a lot of dating chances and a woman has her needs too, you know." Just then the doors opened and they both stood to attention.

Admiral Takeo and Duplex Agens stood in front of them. "What have you got? Is the engines fixed?" The admiral looked expectantly.

"Sir... Thanks to Captain Sarah," Morecambe started.

"It was a team effort," Sarah interjected.

"Alright, so it was a team effort. Go on," the admiral directed, starting to get irritated. Meanwhile, Duplex had a hard time trying to repress a smile while looking at Sarah, who was now blushing.

"Right, sir." Morecambe stammered, getting more nervous. "Thing is, I replaced the parts that were destroyed by the blast from the battle. However, the engines didn't work still, so I been checking everything. With Sarah's help, we discovered both ships have been remotely shut down, sir. We will not be able to move again until the lock is removed." He stood silently.

"Morecambe also discovered who sent the signal. Show them," she said and nudged him.

Morecambe turned and unlocked the display, and they all were able to see that Sweeper, from Dark Imperial Intelligence, sent the shutdown signal.

"Admiral," Duplex spoke up. "Go to the bridge and speak to the new Sweeper. She will be able to get the ship's engines going again... Tell the acting Sweeper the Saber says hi." Admiral Takeo turned on the spot and stormed out, apparently too furious for words, as he punched a hole through the door rather than opening it.

"Sarah, I am going to need you. I have a special mission for you," Duplex stated, looking seriously at her.

"Yes, Saber. Do you need me now?" Sarah asked with an almost pleading look.

Duplex smiled again, glancing at Morecambe... "Well, it was a *team effort*. Alright, one hour, Sarah. No more." Duplex saluted Morecambe and with one more look towards Sarah, she said, "Go easy on him." Then with that, she left.

"What did she mean by that at the end?" he asked. Sarah pounced on him, pulling his Engineer suit down midway, so he couldn't move his arms. Then she kissed him, grabbing both of his cheeks with her hands and kissed fully as her hands slid down his chest, running her fingers through his chest hair.

"I've been without a man for eight years, Morecambe. You better last longer than your attention span." She saw him looking down at her chest, so she grabbed hold of him down below. With a small squeeze, she repeated "You better last longer than your attention span. You are not a minute man, right?"

"Right!" he said in a painful voice as she let go of him. She noticed a dark corner with no one around, so she pulled him with her, dragging him by his suit. Then she pushed him into the corner and pounced on him once again.

Noticing a cable cutter on the side table, she grabbed it and cut his suit right down the middle. To tease him and make him sweat, she started to cut over his bulge very slowly. Now, although he was still technically wearing the suit, it was split in two up the front, revealing the body of a man.

His erection bounced up in front of her face as she cut open the suit. Her eyes beamed as she quickly looked up at him as she took him in her mouth, surrounding the firm thick and long erection. She used her saliva to be able to slide her mouth along his length. She felt him touch the back of her throat as she took it all in and started to gag. Morecambe, feeling every part of his body being pleasured as she continued to suck on him, placed his hands on her head, while his mouth hung open, speechless.

Sarah took her time enjoying this, seeing his eyes. "Oh, I am sorry, you wanted to eat!" She had unzipped the suit she was wearing so as soon as she stood up it stayed on the floor and the pants to the uniform dropped to her ankles. She pulled him out from the corner and swapped places with him, so now her back was up against the wall. She pushed him down to his knees.

"Here you go, enjoy. You tasted great; least I can do is let you eat. You are going to need your strength," she said seductively as she forced his head into her groin. Morecambe went straight to work. She was already so wet; he started to suck on her, tasting some of her as he began using his tongue to penetrate her while using his nose to rub the outer part where she was most sensitive.

She let him enjoy himself for a while, but not too long. They only had fifty minutes left. She pulled him up by the arms, put her arms around his shoulders, and kissed him once more, this time tasting herself on his lips. Her hands slowly moved down as Morecambe's hands were at the base of her back enjoying the kiss. As soon as she reached his ass she drove him in between her legs and felt his erection go inside her, stimulating every sense in her body as it burst into fire.

"Fuck me, dammit!" she shouted.

Not that he needed any encouragement, he started to thrust into Sarah with her bracing herself against the wall. She adjusted herself with him still inside of her and wrapped her legs around his waist as he continued to press her up against the wall, allowing him to penetrate hard, fast... and deep. Sarah buried her face into the side of Morecambe's neck as it started to feel great.

"Oh, fuck yeah, I fucking love cock," she shouted out. "You stop now, I'll slice your dick off," she shouted, sweat dropping from her forehead.

Morecambe's body was firm and well-built with his six foot body, dark hair, and six pack abs. Sweat dripped from every pore making his body glow. Strangely, she found seeing him like this, dirty and sweaty, turned her on even more. The engineers never needed to work out like the military did; the work an engineer does can shape a body just as well.

Sarah, as she was getting hot, untied the buttons to her shirt and shoved Morecambe's face into her chest, between her breasts.

"Here you go, you liked looking at them earlier." She moaned more as he started to lick and bite softly on her nipple while continuing to thrust hard into her. She spanked his ass.

"Harder, dammit!" He obeyed as she screamed and screamed loud until she exploded all over him. This continued on and on, not wasting a single minute of that hour.

~

In a long dark corridor, completely black, where one could not see anything beyond the walls of each eight-foot by ten-foot room. Each was a cell with no lights, except for a little glow light near the toilet and the hard shelf that served as a bed, despite not having a mattress. The floor was tiled, while the walls bare and blank, not allowing any light to be reflected.

This was the Dark Intelligence Prison section, where suspects and criminals were held, detained, questioned, and executed. Even if you managed to get out of the cell, you would not be able to see your own feet and hands. There was no light at all, so not even night vision glasses would be of use to you. The guards would turn the lights on when bringing in a new prisoner. Though if a Dark Knight was bringing in a prisoner, they would use the Dark Power, with the Dark Guards and Dark Royal Guards, the Emperor had made their helmets be able to use some of that Dark Power to see through the Dark Fog.

Because that was what, how and why there was no light. The Fog, which surrounded the Emperor, if you were ever lucky enough to see the Emperor, is designed to block out all forms of light. It is physical, unlike a meteorological fog, and it can contain powers. For instance, with this particular fog, if you touched it, it would let everyone in the Intelligence building and Dark Knight citadel know a prisoner was out of their cell.

Prisoners could not even see four feet in front of them, so the guards and security would already be there before a prisoner even took their first step.

This was the high security section for high profile prisoners, such as the new occupant in cell twelve beta, Sweeper.

Sweeper was just sitting on the bed with her knees up, elbows on her knees, and her face in her hands. The first four hours she could not stop crying from the shock. Then came anger. She walked up to the entrance of her cell too fast and walked into a fire field. Luckily, it was just a warning, only giving her a small jolt of heat. She knew repeated attempts would make it increase the temperature until it burnt her. This was her prison.

"I don't know what to do; I don't know what I am supposed to have done," she said to herself. "It could not of been me who sent that message, the one Tyrik said I sent. Why don't they realize after what I went through to gain the trust of Cryptic M? Do they think I would turn traitor? What? Because he died, they think my loyalties died with him?" she answered her own question. No one else was around. She knew no one else would be in this section.

"I need to get out of here and find out what really is going on. Who has my codes? They would have to be the old codes before they gave me the new ones." She punched the wall in frustration. "White Knight, dammit, this is not fair."

Bored again, she unbuttoned her pants and her hand slid down. There was nothing else to do besides sleep and masturbate. This was the umpteenth time she had pleasured herself.

"I would kill the fucking General on Rriban if they needed me to," she sighed as she relaxed and started to get into it more.

"You want the chance?" said a strange, yet familiar, voice. This made Sweeper jump, startled and blushing with embarrassment. "Would you like me to wait until you are finished? I know you enjoyed watching Tyrik and I in the shower?" Killtooth stepped forward, lowered the fire field, and entered her cell. He turned around putting the field back up again.

He was carrying a small flash light. Sweeper went to do up her pants. "NO! Stop right there. In fact, take them off," Killtooth ordered.

"What?!" she protested.

Killtooth stepped forward. "You watched us; now, I want to watch you enjoy yourself. We are going away after this and I don't want you with all that pent-up aggression where you snap again. Here, drink this." He put a flask in her hands. She took a sip and instantly drank the contents, Cuvee van de Keiser.

"Right, now though you are a prisoner and I am a Dark Knight, you will listen to me. Drop your pants and continue to enjoy yourself. I am ordering you to relax. I will not harm you. I know what has happened to you, Tyrik told me. We, as in you, Tyrik and I, have a mutual friend," he said.

Sweeper sat back down on the bed. Feeling a little more relaxed, she sat with her back against the wall and legs open, and she continued to rub herself, letting Killtooth look. He was shining the flash light directly at her groin.

"So you enjoyed watching us then?" he asked her.

"I did. Seeing Tyrik inside of you was hot," she said as she was arousing herself.

"Good," he smiled. "I heard you saying you need to get out of here, to find out who is framing you. Are you sure you want this? I mean, you can leave it up to the army and the investigation to find you innocent. Would you want the chance to kill the Republic on Rriban, or is that part of your frustration? While you are in here, you are safe; if you go out, we cannot protect you like we can here, which was why you were put into a high security area. It doesn't look good for you right now though…"

He stopped as he could tell she was about to climax. She started moaning loud as she came on her fingers.

"Can I get my pants on now?" she asked. As an answer, he flashed the light up and down to signal that she could.

"My Lord, I am so angry right now. I could kill anyone right about now if the Emperor ordered me to." She stood up and, formality put aside, she hugged him.

"Ha, Tyrik warned me you were a hugger. He's right; your hugs are nice." His hard ass exterior melted away as he hugged her back. "This is why I wanted you to do what you just did. You are no good to anyone when in a rage. Anger is good, so you needed to relax just a little to bring you down from rage to angry. Oh, don't get me wrong, I enjoyed it." He stepped back, holding both of her hands. "This is your point of no return, you can never be Sweeper again if you come with me. You understand?"

"Who is the friend?" she asked.

"You will find out if you come with me," he stated.

"What we doing still standing here?" With that, she picked the Sweeper name tag off her shirt and placed it on the shelf where there was a nice wet spot.

Then they both turned and exited the cell. Killtooth led with the now ex-Sweeper of Dark Imperial Intelligence in hand, as she could not see anything.

# CHAPTER 11

The explosion high in the orbit had made everyone stand still and look up, Republic and non-Republic alike. Burning bodies could be seen falling from the sky. The ship was still in orbit on the fringes of space, however, there was enough oxygen left to allow the fire to breathe. Standing behind Biaci was Captain David, who had just witnessed the Dark Knight Master press the button on the remote he had made for her.

She turned and they both stared at each other. However, Captain David remained silent, stunned into silence as Biaci walked past and placed the remote into his hand, simply saying, "Great work, it worked like a charm."

She walked down the stairs and back out onto the streets to greet her Apprentice. She walked over to her. Although the relationship was supposed to be that of Master and student, it somehow transcended into much more. Maybe it was because they were both women or they shared a moment during Fortis' surgery. Perhaps during her fight with Lt. Powell, Biaci had felt everything Fortis was feeling.

The personnel at the barricade were in tremendous cheer as Fortis climbed over to everyone hugging her, patting her on her back, and looking at her new foot. Her dad was waiting for her, and hugged her. Then Fortis saw her master standing isolated from the crowd, just waiting for her. She ran up to her into a full hug, which Biaci welcomed and returned. Fortis buried her face in Biaci's chest. Biaci could hear the tears finally starting to flow from Fortis' eyes.

Keeping a firm grip on Fortis, she turned her back to the crowd and led Fortis into the building where they had held Jere. Having reached the room, Biaci helped her into a chair and walked over to a wooden keg. They were all out of Duplex's Dead Rise. Instead they had Hitachino, a white ale, also created on Rriban, which Biaci had come to love over time. She poured some of the drink into a small glass and handed it to Fortis.

Biaci wasn't worried; she knew Fortis could handle herself. She had killed already. Biaci was more concerned with how she was able to use her new foot so quickly, not even an hour after having it attached. Then she was dealing with the issue of Powell.

However, all that would have to wait. Both of the doctors knocked on the door and entered without waiting.

"Forgive us, you are needed outside immediately. An Imperial ship is coming. We can look after Fortis," Fortis' dad said.

Sighing Biaci stood up, unclipped the hilt to her brother's fire saber, and handed it to Fortis. "You are my apprentice, your training has already started."

She left as the doctors were putting a blanket over Fortis. Apparently, she was going into shock now that the adrenaline was wearing off.

Biaci went out to the sounds of an engine loud overhead. She reached inside her chest guard and recovered the ear piece she had used for Duplex. "This is Dark Knight Master Biaci, to the unidentified Imperial ship. You receive me?"

The voice of Captain Jarad came through her ear piece, "Yes, my Lord, compliments of Sweeper. You have a place for us to land?" The co-ordinates were transmitted and the ship started to land.

"My Lord, have your engineers join you when you come. You need to start taking this ship apart and setup the guns and missile launchers where you need them. Also, my Lord, I have strict orders to put you in front of my radio, on the double." His voice trailed off as the ship began the landing procedure.

"CAPTAIN DAVID!" Biaci shouted. "CAPTAIN DAVID! CAPTAIN JACK! To me, on the double, bring your engineers. Make sure there is someone to cover the barricade. Order them to report to me soon as they see the enemy doing anything. They would of seen the ship as well."

She went running back into the room to fetch her Apprentice, and she opened the door seeing the doctors attending to her. "Apprentice, stand to. I know you need time, however, we have reinforcements. Doctors, make a list of supplies needed and head over to the ship."

Fortis stood up, instantly stating, "Master, I believe I know what my individual power is." They turned to start moving towards the ship.

"Which is?" Biaci replied.

"I am able to syphon or borrow the powers of other power users nearby. I felt you watching me; I can't explain it, but I did not feel pain at all. I know that is your ability, Master." She looked up to her Master, but she didn't get a reply for a few moments.

"Let's confirm it," she finally responded. "Can you borrow some of my speed?" Biaci instantly jumped into a sprint; the excitement of visitors got to her.

At first, Fortis, frustrated, failed to replicate what happened earlier. However, she thought of her Master and felt it begin; the speed in her feet was automatic. As she started running at the same speed as Biaci, she quickly caught up as they both arrived at the landing pad, just in time for them to see the loading ramp being lowered. It wasn't even all the way down when both, Master and Apprentice, jumped onto it and ascended the ramp.

"Captain Jarad!" Biaci remarked, as she shook his hand. "My apprentice, Fortis." She gestured. "Behind me will be my Captains and their engineering crews. Where is your radio?" The captain pointed and not saying anything else, she waved to her apprentice to follow.

She reached down to the radio station. "Dark Seeing Eye, Dark Seeing Eye, this is Rriban. You receive?" She repeated this once more.

"This is Sweeper of Dark Intelligence. Who am I speaking to?" Sweeper reported.

"Dark Seeing Eye, we are talking in the open? If so, state the clearance code," she ordered.

"Rriban, this is the Saber," Duplex's came on the radio. "Dark Seeing Eye is blind. Confirmation, Knight initiate Oscar, Romeo, Juliet, Tango, clearance code two, eight, one, three, six, four," Duplex finished stating.

"Code received. This is Dark Knight Master Biaci, also present Apprentice Fortis," Biaci reported.

"New Sweeper is in charge. She is not familiar with all the protocols yet. Old Sweeper been arrested for treason. Report, Dark Knight Biaci," Duplex ordered.

"We are holding strong. We're in a deadlock with the Republic forces, we hold the district with no chance of losing it. Quarter mile no-man's land between us and the intelligence HQ. With the kitchen staff, you liberated a number of medical staff, and other staff members have defected, including Rockwell's staff clerk, who is now my Apprentice.

"We have killed three of Rockwell's commanders: his son, Jere, and my apprentice killed Lt. Powell and Walter. The enemy has been reinforced by the White Knights. We are now setting up defenses with the ship that has just landed. They are tearing apart the ship now.

"We just completed a ceasefire and recovered wounded. I was the reason the hospital ship blew up; it was my apprentice's idea. Commander Rockwell's son had a locator chip, whom we had prisoner. Used him and the ceasefire to make sure they were on that hospital ship.

"I had a remote rigged up to transmit the detonation of his self-destruct that was implanted. Again, my apprentice's idea. Have you made sure they haven't been able to contact the Republic?" she finished reporting.

"This is Sweeper. All communications have been monitored, and thanks to the scout ship in the area, all communications not using the authentication is blocked and denied. Also, the situation report states the White Knight ship had communications destroyed; they will not have any long-range capability. They need to relay the signal, like we are to you, to be able to reach Kaas or Coroscate," Sweeper finished.

"Are you able to send teams to the locations of the planted explosives?" Duplex asked.

"We are pinned in. If either side tries anything, we are gunned down," Biaci replied. "How will you be able to land troops and get to Rockwell before they destroy the planet?" she asked.

"Master, may I speak?" Fortis interjected, not at all nervous.

"Go ahead, they can all hear you," Biaci responded.

"Master, Sweeper, and Emperor's Saber, there is another way to go about solving the problem of the explosives. If you are not sure if you can get to the explosives in time, just kill Rockwell. He has just lost his son, so he is going to be all emotional and not able to maintain his control. So we have the advantage. The reason why that is important is because General Rockwell and only Rockwell has the authority to set off the explosives, so…"

"So," Duplex interrupted. "We kill him, we kill the problem of the explosives. You sure about this? There is no other way they can set off the explosives manually?"

"They respond to authorization codes only, which until they receive, they are paper weights. They're chemical bombs; they are not even armed. Worse case is if while dying, he passes that code to General Chester. Then after Rockwell's death, Chester can give the authorization. However, that is the good thing about being shot; it is rather instantaneous."

 She smiled, which was pointless because only her Master could see. However, she returned the smile as she knew she was imagining the death of Rockwell, who only moments ago allowed her to go free. 'How far she had come in so short of time,' Biaci thought to herself.

"Fortis, you appear to be very powerful. Knight, tell me, what is your individual power?" Duplex questioned.

"I believe it is syphon, Saber. I was able to use my master's abilities just by thinking of her. I only just had surgery to replace my foot, and I used her power to not feel pain as I killed Lt. Powell, who raped me," she finished explaining.

"Apprentice," Duplex stated. It took a moment for Biaci to remember she was still Duplex's apprentice. "I trust that our business can wait until the issue is done with. The Emperor has ordered me to Rriban. I ensure you the Republic nor the White Knights will deny you your chance to fight me. I want us to concentrate on Rriban. Agreed?"

"Agreed, Master. I will be transmitting a request in text. One moment," she responded. Then she typed on the keyboard, too fast for Fortis to see.

"Yes, Apprentice, those ships have the capability of doing that. If they rescue or controlled by one of us, the ship can re-equip us," Duplex Agens replied.

"Captain Jarad!" Biaci said aloud, and the captain came to her presently. Biaci wrote instructions down and handed the note to Captain Jarad. He accepted the note and looked down, then quickly glanced at Fortis and back to Biaci.

"Right, my Lord." He saluted and went off to the far end of the ship where it was still untouched.

"Master," Biaci turned back to the radio. "Is my sister doing okay?"

Duplex laughed in response and smiled to herself. "Yes, your sister helped out with the engineering problem, then she worked out her frustrations from Rriban with the Engineer. She is fitting in fine." She paused for a moment. "Apprentice, we are coming. I am not going to say when because I don't want whoever is listening to know too much. However, we are coming, and soon. Dark Empire out." The communication was over, and with that, Biaci turned off the radio.

Captain Jarad returned with a sealed box and stood at attention. Biaci stood up, looking at it, but didn't take it.

"Apprentice, kneel," Biaci ordered.

"Who you were died with the betrayal of your beloved; your past died with the death of Powell. Danielle, who you once were is dead forever, including everything that happened until now. Everything that happened!" She turned, opened the box Jarad was still holding and lifted out a black outfit.

"Apprentice Fortis, I am proud to confirm you a Dark Knight." She leaned over and placed the robe over Fortis' head, As it rested on her shoulders, Biaci used her knife to cut away all of the other clothes Fortis was wearing, displaying Fortis' very beautiful body.

Captain Jarad, seeing this, became slightly embarrassed and turned his head to face the opposite direction. "It's hot here all of a sudden," he remarked. Both Biaci and Fortis looked at him, smiling as Biaci turned back and let the robe fall into place.

Biaci then went to remove the patch on her left arm. However, as soon as her hand went to touch it, it burned her through the glove, drawing blood from her hand. She saw her patch change from that of an Apprentice to that of a Master Assassin as there were now two drops of blood coming from the hand which was also dark red which was her brothers blood.

"My Lord, in the box," Jarad remarked towards Biaci. All the kill marks on Biaci's right arm had disappeared, and now in the box was a new Apprentice patch. Biaci picked up the patch and the saber hilt that was in the box.

"Apprentice, put the saber I gave you to the side," waiting for her to place the weapon aside, she then fixed the patch to Fortis' left arm with the hand that was bleeding. Yet again, the hand turned dark red, this time with Biaci's blood.

"This saber has been fitted for you," she said, as she presented it to Fortis.

"You are now, hereby, a Dark Knight Apprentice, Fortis. Please turn to face the exit of the ship." Fortis turned to see both her dad and brother witnessing her becoming a Dark Knight.

"Thank you, Jarad." Biaci stated, taking out a small box, but not opening it. "Apprentice, I would like to do this in front of everyone here, however, perhaps this is best. Dr. Slowcombe, please come up. Fortis, although you have only just become an apprentice, much of what we have done has been from your assistance. Your strength, passion and power have not gone unnoticed by me. Confirmed by the Emperor's Saber, hereby in the name of the Emperor, you are being awarded the highest award for bravery, the Red Star Medal. Just as when seeing the sign, it gives us hope. Wherever you go from this day forth, citizens of the Dark Empire will get hope from your presence. Dr Slowcombe, would you like to give your daughter, Fortis, her medal?" she ended, handing him the box.

The very proud father opened the box and saw the small medal, about the size of a large coin, in the shape of the red star. He picked it up from the box and affixed it above the leather chest guard over her right breast.

Standing now on the ship was the transformed Fortis. No longer did she look like Danielle; she wore black leather boots like Biaci, which zipped up to just below the knee, the robe with leather chest guard and breast plates, and a gold belt around her waist over the stomach area bearing the symbol of the Republic being stabbed with a dagger. Fortis noticed the one kill mark on her right arm and knew it was Powell.

"Apprentice, your first order. Use the ship bed, take it where you want and sleep for the next four hours. We will start training when you are awake and have the doctors look at you. Go now, there is nothing else you can do while we get this thing relocated," Biaci ordered.

With that, her father, Dr. Slowcombe, and her brother, Tim, with an arm around her walked off the ship as her dad, with the other doctor's help ,carried the ship's bed.

# CHAPTER 12

On the bridge of the Dragomire, Admiral Takeo had arrived from Engineering. The walk helped him calm down a little, but not by much. He entered the bridge and a worker was crouched down, working to repair a blown circuit breaker. The Admiral didn't wait for him to move, but just walked straight into him, knocking him over. As he stormed onto his Bridge, he demanded, "Get me in contact with Intelligence."

"That will not be necessary," Lord Thant commanded throughout the room.

Taken aback, the admiral was surprised to see him, "My Lord," he said, bowing. "How may I serve the Dark Council?"

"The situation is too important for there not to be a representative of the council here, so I arrived here by shuttle soon as the situation was declared," he explained.

"My Lord, have you not heard?" he started to ask. "Sweeper has been arrested for treason; there is a new Sweeper in place, my Lord."

"Really, that does surprise me; she didn't seem the sort," he replied with all emotion hidden. Just then, the doors to the bridge opened again and the Emperor's Saber entered.

"My Lord," Duplex said. "I am surprised to see you here, given the Emperor's order," she stated.

"I was just explaining to the Admiral, it is too important to not have a representative of the council present. The engines should work now," Thant stated.

"How do you know, my Lord?" she asked, staring directly at him. It did no good; his mind was sealed.

"I had the former Sweeper shut down the engines soon as she announced plan Ban to allow me time to get here. I just sent the code to inform I am here, so whoever is Sweeper should get the go ahead," he said, taking a step forward to try and assert his authority.

"Well, my Lord, the Dragomire is my flag ship. You been given orders to not interfere with me, so you will, if you intend on staying, go to the Morgan Rice. Is that clear?" she ordered.

"Who are you to order me?" Thant retorted, stepping closer, yet again. He was two feet taller than Duplex Agens.

"I am Duplex Agens, Emperor's Saber. And in case you forgot, I don't answer to you, just the Emperor to whom you serve. So unless you want to try to place your own authority over our Emperor, and I believe you are familiar with what happened to the last council members who got too big for their own heads,"—she pointed to the door—"the shuttle to the Morgan Rice is that way."

Lord Thant walked up once more and placed the hilt of his Fire saber under Duplex's chin.

"If you were…" he started to say, but he was interrupted.

"If you going to do it, do it already. Come on, prove you have no regard for the Emperor's words; show everyone you are a traitor by killing the agent of the Emperor's hand," she growled, not even flinching or moving an inch. She would not give Lord Thant the pleasure.

Forcefully, he shoved the hilt hard up and to the left, cutting Duplex's chin. "You've grown too big for your own good, Saber," he said as he walked away.

"Admiral, as the Emperor's Saber, I hereby grant you authority over Lord Thant. You do not, I repeat, do not, take any orders from him or the Dark Council. You will not be punished for it," she ordered.

"What was that all about?" he asked.

"He made a mistake. Is there a way you can talk with the Admiral on the Morgan Rice securely?" she asked, and he nodded in response.

"Good, go start it; I will join you presently. Tell him everything I just told you, including the order; I will be with you to explain further. I need to report this to the Emperor." She walked off as the Admiral went into the office on the other side of the bridge to start the private call. Duplex looking around, and seeing the Ensign, she ordered, " You, Ensign, come here."

Ensign Bollinger dropped what he was doing and reported on the double, standing to attention in front of Duplex, "My Lord..." He offered a medical patch for her chin.

"Thank you, Ensign. What is your name?" she asked, taking the patch.

"Ensign Bollinger. They call me Baby Face, my Lord, but Ensign Bollinger is the name," he answered nervously, all too quick.

Duplex smiled, "Well, do you have a group of people you trust?"

"Yes, my Lord, the night watch shift; I'd trust them to the death, my Lord," he replied instantly.

"Good. Computer code: Emperor's saber, Papa, Romeo, Oscar, execute. In the Emperor's name, I hereby grant you, Ensign Bollinger, the rank of Lieutenant. Form your night watch and head down to the shuttle bay instantly. You will need special outfits; they will be provided to you on the shuttle that has already been marked out" Duplex finished ordering. with the sound in the background of the computer Promotion confirmation Bollinger, now Lt. Bollinger presently on Dragomire Bridge,

"Thank you, my lord." He bowed, then saluted and then went to summon his night watch group and head out. As Duplex went over to the side panel that was remote from everyone else, she entered the saber's code: plus, three, one, three.

The screen went black with the symbol of the hand showing. "My Emperor, Council member, Lord Thant, has arrived unannounced. Did you request he come out here?"

The single word appeared, "No..."

"I have given the order to the Admirals that they ignore any and all commands from Lord Thant. I believe this is the mistake; he stated he told Sweeper to shut down the engines until he got here. What would you want me to do about this?" she asked.

Again, one word displayed, "Wait..." Then it was replaced with, "I have overridden the Sweeper's shutdown command..."

"My Emperor, I have put together the team, ready for the mission. Do you need me with the team itself or with the Army?" Duplex asked.

"Go with the mission; the enemy general must die..." the words appeared and quickly vanished.

"Lord Thant must be punished..." the words came up and then the communication ended.

Admiral Takeo was in the office, sitting at his desk. "Admiral, you are going to be getting a visitor from the Council, Lord Thant. Emperor's Saber's orders are to ignore Lord Thant; you and I have authority over him. Basically making our lives hell because we both know he won't take to that too well."

"Why was this done?" Admiral Soemu asked.

"Because he defied the Emperor's orders; he is not supposed to be here," Duplex reported loudly, as she entered the room.

"We cannot order him to leave. However, we do not have to take any of his orders, in regards to a military sense. That remains squarely under your command still. The Morgan Rice is under your command," she stated. "I have just confirmed it; he is to be made felt uncomfortable. This is the direct orders of the Emperor. If he wants to be here he can stay, however, we will not make it easy for him. So the same order goes for you Soemu, Lord Thant has no power or authority over you for the duration of this mission."

She walked over and sat down at the opposite side of the desk. "Admirals, it is time. After this conversation is over, start the count down. Forty eight hours. Then come with everything, I have been assigned the task of preventing them from destroying the planet before we can secure it. Gentleman, the next time we speak, we will be once again on Rriban. Oh, Admiral Takeo, I have promoted Bollinger. I will be borrowing his night watch shift, hope you do not mind."

"By all means, you can have Baby Face." He stood up and offered his hand, and Duplex took it. "For the Empire, for the Emperor," they both said, as Duplex left the room. The clock had started.

# CHAPTER 13

"Gentleman, we find ourselves in a unique situation here," General Chester stated. Once again, they were in the briefing room, quite noticeably minus Commander Rockwell. The news of the Centaur destruction, which had meant the death of his son, had driven Rockwell into a state of mental collapse and shock.

Therefore, General Chester was once again in charge, along with Commanders Douglas and William, and the White Knights Sergio and Ramon.

"Allow me to get this out of the way, with the size of the force Master Sergio reported that intercepted him, we have to assume they are coming here. I do not believe we can hold the planet. So we could start the evacuation now and save what we have left," Chester finished announcing.

"Sir," Douglas spoke up. "I'm not running from them; mainly, there is not enough room on Sergio's ship for all of us. I suggest, as it is still imperative to get word back to Coroscate, we need to crush this resistance fast before the invasion comes, if possible."

"Sir," William interjected. "Please extend our sympathies to Commander Rockwell for his loss. However, with him being incapacitated, we cannot contemplate leaving the planet; we cannot allow this planet to fall back into their hands. Right now, only Rockwell can make sure that happens. They know this, so I insist, if Ramon would oblige us,"—he smiled and nodded politely towards Ramon—"We need a detail of White Knights around Rockwell; he is going to be a target for assassination."

"We can take over the Non-Republic district."—everyone stopped to look at Sergio—"From everything I have heard, we need three things to happen. One, get word back to Coroscate, so to that effect, we will transfer the entire crew of my ship, except for essential positions. Then transfer your personnel that you believe to be '*soft*'—I believe is how I heard Commander Douglas describe them—to my Ship. Send the ship off, without delay, before they come. We will leave all ships and shuttles, and land them on the planet. You will have like three hundred White Knights, which we can crush that district with. Just because we may not win and we have to destroy the planet, it will be prudent to send the ship, so in any event, The Republic will know at least they are alive."

"Master Sergio, would it not be best to keep the ship here to defend the planet? You should be able do some damage; destroying one of their dreadnaughts or slowing them down will do a lot to help us," queried White Knight Ramon, the leader of the White Knights on Rriban.

"Master, if the ship stayed, it would be a waste. They have upgraded their ships since we last fought; my ship is no match for their two dreadnaughts," he replied.

"I like Master Sergio's idea. We're not assuming we will fail, however, I like the insurance that someone will know what is going on back here. Master Ramon, will your forces join in with Sergio?" General Chester asked.

Ramon nodded his confirmation.

"Okay, that part is settled. Masters Ramon and Sergio, please go carry out that order. We need to get that ship off before they come." The order was given, and with that, both White Knights turned and left to start the preparations.

"Now, is there any other way we can set off the explosives or can we come up with our own?" Chester put the open question out to the remaining officers.

"No, sir, we do not have enough explosives, and even if we did they would not work. The explosives needed are the ones chosen, and they will not do anything until the chemicals react. Sir, when is the point where we set off the explosives? If we don't have a chance of holding them off, why not now?" William responded to the open question.

Douglas interjected, "Because we are going to make them pay for every inch they want back." Just then, the door opened up and Rockwell entered. His face looked like a ghost, pale and white, with no hint of color.

Everyone stopped to look at him.

"Sorry, gentleman, for my lateness. The new doctor has given me a clean bill of health. I won't be taking command just yet, but I refuse to sit in bed while the fate of this planet is being decided." Using a walking cane, he went over to one of the chairs and sat down.

"Commander Rockwell, we appreciate you being here; we are all very sorry for the loss of your son. We've established a plan. We are going to transfer the White Knight crew to the planet and the non-combatants up to the ship, and send the ship back to Coroscate. The White Knights will crush that district—" General Chester was interrupted.

"I will be leading that assault," Rockwell said.

"With respect, you will not," Chester retorted. "You are the only one who can set off the demolitions."

"Which is exactly why I must go. The enemy knows this too, so when they see me in front, they must assume that has changed. I am instructed to give the codes to the next senior officer if I am going to die, so this is what I will do. If they kill me, they will not know who will be in charge and who has the capability to set off the charges, giving us the upper hand. Also, my General, I need to speak to you privately. We have a friend behind their lines," Rockwell stated confidently.

The commanders all stared at him with serious looks. "You are assuming they will kill you. You do not have a locator chip, so you could be killed and we will never know. On the other hand, they could capture you. The commands would only respond to General Chester if you are dead," Douglas spoke out.

"In that case, make sure that I am. You will have every single shuttle planet side. They only have one gun platform. Send all the shuttles and obliterate the district. I am doing this; the only way you can stop me is if you shoot me now. Arresting me will not help, the guards are on my side; I've paid them off and they want revenge for the Centaur. The White Knights, with me leading them, is our best chance."—he stood up— "You have no choice! Except for the choice of killing me now, or let it be done by the enemy."

Just then, the door opened up. Master Sergio walked back in and saluted General Chester.

"Sir, transfer is under way. The White Knights on my ship have already started to land planet side. The people waiting to be sent to the ship have been ordered to report to the landing pads. We will be complete in thirty minutes," he reported.

"Master Sergio, Commander Rockwell is insistent on leading the charge, ahead of the White Knights. Your recommendations?" General Chester asked.

Master Sergio took a sideward glance in Rockwell's direction, then back to General Chester. "I will double his guard, sir. I would suggest he trade his current uniform of the Republic to that of a White Knight. It will send a strong message to them, sir."—he glanced toward Rockwell again— "Sir, it is clear there is no stopping him. I will not shoot him and make it easy for the enemy; give them the task of killing him."

"Very well. Your request is… reluctantly approved. Commander Rockwell, during the attack, you may retain your rank of General," General Chester ordered. "Meeting is adjourned."

With that, the commanders both stood up and left, leaving Sergio and Rockwell. They both walked up to General Chester.

"Sir, this is the plan and our friend is now currently listening…" Rockwell started to say.

~

"My Lady!" Captain David reported to Biaci and saluted.

"What is it, Captain?" Biaci replied. She was joined by Captain Jarad and the doctors, who were going over the placements for the medical supplies from Jarad's ship.

"My Lady, heavy activity from the Republic side has been observed. They are sending ships and shuttles to the land and back up to the ship in orbit, counted sixty ships so far. There is also extra build-up in their lines. They've intensified their front lines, so we cannot see beyond few lines of infantry. I suspect they are going to attack, and soon," Captain David finished reporting.

" Captain Jarad," Biaci asked. "Are the guns in place and working?"

"Yes, my Lord. All guns are in place, however, I took the precaution seeing you only have one gun battery. so I turned one weapon into an anti-aircraft gun. The position was just too exposed otherwise," Jarad replied.

"Captain David, proceed to the radio and report we suspect the attack to begin soon. Ask what they recommend, if we should fight a holding action or if we should break out," she ordered. She saluted Captain David as he ran off to carry out the order.

Biaci and Captain Jarad proceeded on walking, leaving the doctors. At the sound of battle coming, the physicians instantly stopped talking about new supplies and started organizing what they had for the incoming patients they knew would be coming.

"If they plan to attack, they are going to need enough to punch through the fire power we've had before; any tanks they've sent, I've been able to stop and watch them being destroyed." Biaci started to laugh.

"I apologize, I don't see what is funny," Captain Jarad said, smiling at her.

"Oh," she said, realizing he didn't understand. Smiling back, she explained, "I was just reminded of something my Master told me, and I told my sister. I just caught myself, doing, which is what made me laugh. There is endless possibilities of what they could be doing, each as likely as the other. Do not try to predict what, that is the enemy jobs, and they will tell you soon enough." They had walked up to the top of their tallest building to observe the battle lines. "So, Captain, let us not worry about what they will do; let us worry about how, where, and why." She stopped at the edge.

"Well, the 'where' is easy; the only point of access there is, is across the no man's land. Also, by air," Jarad stated.

"Right, Captain, so how about the 'how' and 'why'?" she asked, testing him, as she looked out towards the battle lines again.

"By using their best troops, the only thing that explains those shuttles, Master. They are going to use their White Knights," Fortis said. The quiet shy voice of Danielle had completely gone, replaced with a strong dominant voice.

She walked up slowly.

"Is that all?" Biaci asked, not showing any sign of acknowledgement of Fortis. Captain Jarad, however, turned, saluted, and bowed slightly before returning to standing at attention.

"They could easily use the dreadnaught guns to fire at us. However, they have not so far, so that tells me they want to capture, not destroy, which gives us the advantage," Fortis replied.

"Oh... How so, Apprentice?" Biaci asked her again with a commanding tone of voice.

"Rockwell is no longer in charge. Otherwise, we wouldn't be here talking now. If he were, he'd want revenge, and when you want revenge, you don't stop for anything until your target is dead. When you are trying to capture, you have to hold back your full strength. Else you may kill what you hope to capture, Master." She stood still behind her master.

"They are also desperate, Apprentice. Right now, they have to be feeling the heat of our fleet. Their dreadnaught crew had to of told them what they saw, so they know. Plus, there is still a traitor, so chances are they know everything we intend to do."—she looked down—"The people on the Centaur died for nothing, Apprentice. It just delayed what they are trying to do now." She turned to look at her Apprentice.

"It is foolish to think they would never find out what is going on here, Master; all we can do is slow them down. Master, you need to speak to your master about this. They have to be informed because only they will be in a position to do anything with an incoming attack. We will be too busy to deal with their ship, which, Master, I believe answers your 'why' question," Fortis responded, as she turned to Jarad.

"Captain Jarad," Fortis said. "I suggest you use the regular ammunition your guns used when they were still part of your ship."

"We are going to need that much fire power? Won't that be slight overkill?" Captain Jarad asked.

"Captain,"—Biaci turned to look at him—"each shuttle coming from the ship is a shuttle full of White Knights."

"Right!" Jarad exclaimed, as he ran off to make the switch of ammunition, leaving just the Master with her Apprentice.

Biaci walked forward, keeping her apprentice on her right side. Fortis was looking toward the battle lines.

Suddenly Biaci jumped in with a sideward attack with her fire saber. Fortis avoided by stepping forward and she spun around to her right, not even drawing her own fire saber.

Landing on her feet again, Biaci came in with a strike toward Fortis' head, but Fortis finally drew her own saber and blocked the strike with a strike of her own, knocking Biaci's blade back. Fortis, with both hands, grabbed Biaci's robe and sat down, making her and Biaci roll backwards. Biaci was pinned to the floor with Fortis on top.

However, mid maneuver, Biaci used the Dark power to send Fortis flying off her. Fortis had to somersault forward to counter the push, so she was not sent flying off the roof top. Instead, she landed back on the building's roof top, splintering the stone tiles as she landed.

Fortis focused on Biaci; using her own power, she started to borrow one of Biaci's powers.

Biaci, taking this pause to mean Fortis was getting tired, went in for the charge using her force speed. She moved side to side. If Fortis had blinked, she would have missed her. Just as Biaci came out of the speed run, Fortis saw her coming in with a stabbing thrust. Fortis made sure her arm was there to meet it as Biaci's blade went straight through Fortis right bicep.

Fortis grabbed the hilt from Biaci's hand, with Biaci's blade still in her arm. She tripped up Biaci, making her fall to the ground. Then Fortis held the tip of her blade at Biaci's throat.

"Do you yield master?" Fortis questioned, panting as she tried to catch her breath.

"You are fighting a power user, not a regular foot soldier," Biaci replied. As she raised her hand, her saber flew out of Fortis' right bicep and back into its owner's hand. She used it to knock the fire saber out of Fortis' hand and tripped her at the same time as she was getting up. Fortis fell to a knee. Biaci stepped a foot down on Fortis' saber and placed her own saber under Fortis' chin, as she stepped around behind Fortis, holding an arm around her.

"You fought well today, Apprentice." She turned off her saber. " If you going to use my power, I guess I should give you the same warning I got. Do not make promises your body can not keep. You are going to run out of body parts if you keep up like that, and you may get stabbed in a more vital part. Pain can be a good thing; lets you know you are not dead ."

"I should of stopped your saber coming out of my arm," Fortis said bitterly, as she picked up her saber.

"If you had, you'd be looking for a new arm to match your foot. Do not be hasty to become all machine," Biaci  reprimanded. "It is okay to do what you did to an extent, but only when there is no other option and you are outmatched. You are at least equal to me, not out classed or out matched, Apprentice, so keep your body parts that you can, while you can. I hope you get to enjoy the pleasures of your body," she said, with a wink.

"Arrrgh!" Fortis suddenly went to one knee again as she started to cradle her arm.

"That is the other part, Apprentice. I could of blocked you from using my power, leaving you where you are now, …hmph," Biaci sighed. "Come on, let's go see your dad." Biaci grabbed Fortis under her left arm, helped her up, and they walked off to find Dr. Slowcombe.

"Master, I'm eager for the battle to come. I am excited for them to see what I have become, thanks to you." —she looked at her master—"Is it wrong for me to want the battle and not be afraid?"

"This is going to be your first major battle. Moments before, your nerves will kick in then. Everything else has been skirmishes. Although we have all these guns and weapons, it will be useless. It is going to be just us two fighting, if they send in White Knights. Nothing else will compare to what we are about to face. The closest I've been to anything like this was when I was still a Reader, and I had to watch it happen on the displays back in Intelligence. I remember I was terrified. The only thing in the end that stood between me and death was my brother.  You and I will be able to hold them off, and the weapons will help to slow them up and even kill a few while we fight them. However, everyone here will not stand a chance if we fail. There will be no more training until it happens, you understand? You need to rest. You will be exhausted if you survive."—Biaci paused and looked up at her Apprentice—"No, it is not wrong. You just do not have the experience to feel anything else. Go spend time with your dad and brother; it may be the last time you see them. I'm going to report to my master."

# CHAPTER 14

Killtooth was at the controls of a modified ship, already laid out and prepared to take off at Kaas City. The ship was similar to the Cryptic ships flown by Cryptic agents employed by the Dark Imperial Intelligence. This ship, however, was provided by their mutual friend. The ship, he could tell, had engine power unlike anything else he had ever seen.

The jolt, as the ship got up off the struts, felt like a kick in the stomach while being punched in the face. He knocked a couple of droids and the refueling truck over before he finally got a grip and lifted the ship up and out of the Dark Knight Citadel. The Dark Knights normally just used the spaceport like anyone else. However, on occasion, they can use their own port. There was nothing really special about it, except everyone seeing the ship take off knew it was Dark Knight business ordered by the Dark Council, seeing as how you needed their permission to be able use the port. The ship hovered above the Citadel. When he activated the ship's main ability and turned the panels on, the outside of the ship also turned on and started to reflect, turning into mirrors. It made the ship appear invisible, as anyone on the outside would just see a reflection.

Killtooth took the ship up and out of the atmosphere of Kaas, then hit the jump to meet up with their destination that had been pre-entered into the ship's computer. He put the computer's auto-navigate on and just sat back. Then a hand appeared over his right shoulder holding a cup. Killtooth gratefully took the cup, sipped, and smiled as he stood.

"Cuvee van de Keiser. Hah, I think you may be addicted..."—Killtooth paused—"What do I call you now? Unless you want to be known as ex- or former-Swecper?" he asked.

They walked off to the main deck area of the ship. The ship's interior was where the similarities to a Cryptic ship stopped. The ship was decorated like a mini floating hotel, with very comfortable chairs and tables with holo-graphic entertainment systems, meaning dancers. A bar was located to the right as you walked into the main area from the flight control deck. The ship could hold up to twenty eight people comfortably, but it could hold a lot more than that, if needed. The medical facility on this ship is located where the conference room would be on a Cryptic ship; this ship's conference or meeting room was located upstairs. There was a spiral staircase that led up to what looked like an observation deck. The roof was actually solid metal like the rest of the ship, however, the technology made it appear as a glass roof, allowing people to have a complete three hundred and sixty degree view from the top of the ship. Apparently, while the ship's stealth was on, it turned on this effect in the meeting room.

The table was round and fairly large, with eight leather chairs surrounding its edge. The carpet on the floor was black, except for a large Red star underneath the table, with each of the points directed at a chair.

The corners held the Dark Knight and Dark Empire flags. The only thing the ship was missing was any guns, a fact that the former Sweeper noticed as soon as she got on this ship.

"You know, I don't exactly enjoy this pleasure yacht of yours, being this is a time of war…" she started to say.

"Sometimes speed is more important than stopping to fight. This is more of a control vessel, where any military commander can observe and make strategic commands without being interrupted by the annoying battle itself.  Besides, you didn't answer my question," Killtooth replied, pushing the point as he sat down.

"For good reason. When will we meet our mutual friend? Where are we going?" she joined him at the table, sitting opposite him.

"We are going to meet another friend, and our mutual friend is on the ship already… Just sit down and relax!" he said quickly, but she stood up as soon as he said that.

"What? Why? Where is he or she?" He had peaked her interest.

"I know you are normally the person to know everything and this is very strange to you, not knowing anything that is going on. It needs to be like this; less you know, the better, right now. Our friend, a fellow Dark Knight, is helping this ship get to the intercept location faster. While we are sitting here, the ship is going about triple the speed a normal ship could go without his help," he stated.

"Without his help…" she repeated. "So, it is a guy?"

"White Knight, dammit, you really don't miss anything, do you?" he said, annoyed.

"You need to stay sharp if you want to keep secrets from a master secret keeper," she said, laughing out loud.

"Is that why you offered the drink? To dull me?" he asked, as he took another sip.

"No, because I saw this ship required a little more handling than most, and you looked like you needed it." she responded, smiling while taking another sip of her drink.

"We can enjoy some of the entertainment while we wait; we have like thirty minutes. There are some male dancers," Killtooth said, gesturing to the table.

"Stop trying to distract me. Answer me. Tell me what we are doing, or tell me what you can." She put her drink down on the table.

"Why should I, since you will not give me a name?" he replied back.

"Why is it so important?" she replied with a worried look.

"I would just like to know what to refer to you by; Sweeper was a title, not a name," he said, looking concerned.

"Yes, it was; we have no identity," she said quietly. "I was Reader Eight, then promoted to Sweeper, and that became my name."

"You wasn't always with the Intelligence; you were working for the other side. You must have had a name then?" She shook her head in response.

"My parents were arrested moments after my birth before they even gave me a name. They were so strict with that sort of thing and they had no sentiment or softness to allow my mother to give me a name before they arrested her. It was the White Knights who told me when I was four… that they were both Knights, they broke the law by having me, and were executed." She bowed her head, hiding her face from Killtooth.

"Well, that is a predicament. Sort of makes you a perfect secret agent, as you are, literally, a person with no identity. Tyrik passed this to me for you." —he presented a small wrapped bundle to her—"He said he knew he was important to you."

She unwrapped the bundle and saw the framed picture of Cryptic M. This broke her down and Killtooth could see the tears falling down her cheek.

"Are you about to hug me again?" he said sarcastically. He had barely finished the sentence when she flung herself at him, wrapping her arms around his shoulders.

"I'm sorry," he said, hugging back. "At least anything you do now will trump anything and everything you've done until now."

She pushed herself away from him. "Again, please tell me something or stop teasing me." She looked up at him with a very pleading look.

"I am not supposed to say anything. I am under very strict orders; you said so yourself back there. You would kill the enemy General on Rriban if the Emperor ordered you to." He stood up, walking away so his back was facing her.

"So we are going to Rriban?" she inquired.

"Right now, all you need to know is we are flying to a pre-determined location, chosen by our mutual friend, where another friend will meet us." With that, he walked off into the crew deck to his room and locked the door behind him.

The woman, former-Sweeper, was left there holding the picture of Cryptic M, the only man she had ever loved. She finished her drink and then retired to her own room.

She looked at her reflection in the tall mirror hanging on the back of her door. Her hair was done up in a tight ball, as per the Dark Imperial Intelligence regulations, and she was still wearing the uniform. Looking at herself, she reached up behind her head, untied the bun, and let her long brown hair fall down around her shoulders as she shook her head. Leaning forward, she kept pushing her hair up with her hands, trying to give it some volume. When she stood up again, her hair reached just below her shoulder blades.

She was bored with how she looked. "Just who are you?" she asked her reflection. She placed the picture of Cryptic M on the side table.

She chose an outfit from the large selection in her closet. A red two-tone Bardot long sleeve top had caught her eye, along with black Power Pont leggings. She set them aside on the bed. She remembered having fun in the tavern with Tyrik and Killtooth; that was the woman she wanted to be. She quickly stripped down and got into the shower, still wondering, what could be planned for her.

Killtooth was right; she was so used to being in control. The fact that now she was not in control, at all, scared her a little bit. She turned the water off and pressed the steam dryer to start; instead of the water, warm high-pressured air went to work drying her. Still in the midst of chaos, calm must be kept, so whatever they have set for her, it has to be better than staying in the cell back in Kaas City.

However, it worried her too. She was with Tyrik and Killooth for the initial incident, however, she was at headquarters when someone using her old codes sent the shutdown signal from Intelligence. If not her, who? She had been in the control room with the readers putting Kaas City onto a war footing.

She stepped out of the shower, fully dry now. She picked up all her work clothing, including the nasty issued underwear that was always itching and the issued underwire bra that constantly poked her side, and tossed them into the waste disposal. From there, the clothing would be burnt up, and when the ship came out of stealth, would be projected into space.

She leaned over picking up the long sleeve top and slid it over her head. She felt the soft silk of the top grazing her skin as she pulled it down into place. She instantly felt the freedom of not wearing any bra, as her shoulders were now bare.

The former Sweeper was not a red skin, she always knew, and was put in her place by some of the less polite Dark Knights, who liked to remind her where her place was. It didn't stop her from being her, the regulations of Intelligence did. She had to keep up a façade for the sake of having no identity. If she had died, the Intelligence could have never acknowledged her. She knew her file with all the other agents, fixers, and Cryptic agents would have been sent off to be incinerated. Now, she was out. She could be the woman that got to breathe for five minutes in the tavern.

She sat down on her bed and pulled on the leggings. She jumped up as she pulled them up to her waist. She then stepped into mini leather boots with two inch heels; they went on with the top edge slightly above the ankles.

She went over to the mini table, and using the mirror, she put on some eye shadow, blush, mascara, and finally, lip stick, but first, she needed to do her nails, as she wanted them to match. She stood up, walked back over back to the entrance of the shower, and turned to face the wall which held a small place for one to insert their fingers. First, she had to pick a color. "All I want is a purple color," she said to herself. Looking through the selection, she saw it was not an easy choice, as there were three hundred and sixty different shades of purple.

She finally picked one that she had the matching lipstick for, Midnight Rose. She placed all ten fingers in and felt the ten brushes, all at once, put on the first coat. Air blew on her nails, then the second layer, the color, was applied. Finally, the top coat was brushed on to protect the nails. She decided to go for an ink design, tiny black versions of the Red Star. After her nails were dried again, she felt ten ink pens pressed onto her nails, printing the design onto each nail with a protective smudge-proof coat over top of the ink to protect the design.

Extracting her hands, she had almost completed the transformation, but there was still something missing. She decided to look at her hair. Next to the closet was a machine much like for the nails, however this device was for hair. She selected her choice, to have two of her bangs framing her face dyed blood red, while the rest of her hair would be dyed black.

Suddenly breaking her out of a trance, she started to position herself in the machine when a knock sounded on the door.

"Are you ready? We approaching the destination. What you doing in there? You been like twenty minutes," Killtooth questioned. Had it really been twenty minutes? she thought to herself. It barely felt like five.

"I'm almost ready"—she gave herself one more look—"ah," she said.

Suddenly, she turned around and grabbed a belt with a gold tinted buckle; she put it on around her waist, but after seeing it in the mirror she changed her mind and discarded it on the floor.

"Okay, I'm coming now." She took one last look in the mirror, gulped, and opened the door. Then there was just a loud crashing sound, as Killtooth dropped a food tray to the ground, with his mouth wide open, gaping at her.

"You know you could of just said I looked smashing without actually smashing things. Hehe," she said, as she gave him cheeky smile and stepped by him confidently.

~

The ship finally started to slow down, gradually coming to a stop. Sarah was in Biaci's ship; she arrived at the pre-determined location. Duplex Agens came up to the flight deck and sat down in the radio station.

"What's their ETA, Sarah?" Duplex asked of her.

"They should already be in this system," she replied.

Duplex switched on the radio and started the repeater signal, a solid ping that repeated every thirty seconds.

"Anything yet?" Duplex asked.

"No… wait, yes, something is inbound, but I don't see anything." She leaned forward, half lifting out of her seat and looked out the windows as if she could see anything. "I don't see anything. We are receiving a response to your ping, but I don't see anything."

Duplex flipped the switch and started to speak, "Tiger one to friendly craft, commence docking procedure." The acknowledge signal was received on the display in front of Sarah, six flashes on the flight control.

"Sarah, set the ship for auto-pilot; disable the ship's engines. They will dock with us," Duplex ordered.

"Who will?" Sarah asked.

Duplex got up and walked down to the main area, where she was greeted by the night watch shift, minus Lt. Bollinger though.

"Where is Bollinger?" Duplex asked Waller.

"He wanted to get changed in there; he felt it was appropriate being an officer and all," Waller responded, pointing to the conference room.

Duplex walked over and opened the door to see a half dressed, bent over Bollinger.

"Clearly those who came up with the name Baby Face, never seen you from this angle Lieutenant." She waited for him to get his pants on, while the other members of his crew had a hard time trying not to laugh.

"Sarah, would you call him Baby Face after seeing that?" Sarah approached behind Duplex.

"White Knight wept, I guess he's compensating for the lack of hair on his face." That did it, the crew busted out laughing. Hearing Sarah say that reminded Duplex of Fidus.

"Did you get that from your Brother or he from you?" she said, looking at Sarah.

"What do you mean?" Sarah responded, with a curious look.

"Your brother used to say that all the time before he became a Knight. 'White Knight wept,'" Duplex explained.

"Oh, I don't know, I had no idea." Sarah answered, looking flummoxed.

"Okay," Duplexed ordered, as she turned, "When the man beast has done changing, we will be embarking onto a ship that is currently docking with us. You need be as if you were inside the Dark Citadel itself, you understand?"

"Sorry, no. What is going on? Why are we here?" Cody asked.

"You will find out when we get aboard. You know who I am and whom I serve. That should give you an inkling of what is going on, given the situation we are all in," Duplex answered.

"Okay, sounds good," replied Cody as he stood.

Now, having finished getting dressed, Bollinger stood up, and saluted to Duplex's back, "Sorry, my Lady."

"Do you think you are above these men?" Duplex asked him.

"My Lady, no, I have to be able to order these people to what could be their death. I need to maintain some detachment as well as being their friend, mother, and father figures, all in one," he recited the officer's manual.

"Right, you are. We'll leave it at that then." Duplex winked, as she could tell the real reason why he wanted to change. She leaned over to whisper in his ear, "Man Beast sounds much more manlier than Baby Face; it will scare off the enemy and it will get the women interested in you." She stood up and tapped on his shoulder.

As she did, the entire ship shuddered and loud clanking sound erupted.. "This will be our ship we are waiting for," Duplex stated.

"My Lady," Sarah said with a sense of urgency, "there is still no ship out there. Look." The entire night watch crew, Bollinger included, ran to the same vantage point as Sarah.

Duplex opened the inner airlock hatch, then with her Saber hilt, she tapped -.. .- .-. -.- .

"You're sending Morse code, you just tapped 'Dark,'" Bellis said.

"Very good, Private," Duplex stated.

Then a response, ...-- .---- ...--, which made Bellis gulp.

"What is it, Bellis?" Cody demanded.

"Three, one, three," Bellis explained.

"Well, that settles that. There has to be someone outside to be able to reply," Waller stated, walking forward confidently.

"Yes, clearly," Bellis said. "Don't you guys know what 'three, one, three' means?"

"I suggest you keep that information to yourself for another fourteen minutes, Private," Duplex ordered.

Killtooth put the wrench aside as he opened the hatch to see the face of the Emperor's saber.

"My Lord, welcome aboard." He offered a hand down, which was taken and he helped Duplex Agens climb up the ladder.

As soon as she got up and stood, she noticed the bomb shell that was looking half nervous, half furious at her.

"Sweeper, oh, I'm sorry, former-Sweeper," Duplex corrected herself. The others started to climb up. "You do look good. Is this the real you coming out?" she said with a smile. The former Sweeper didn't say anything. "Killtooth, didn't you tell her?"

"No, my Lord, was told to refer to you as a friend," he said, half distracted.

"My dear, it's okay. Your friend, Tyrik, told me about your party night with him and Killtooth."—this made Killtooth snap to attention—"I ordered him to tell me; he betrayed no confidence, Killtooth. Good for you, Sweeper!"—She turned, beaming at her—"Uh, there I go again, what would you like me to call you now? Killtooth, as I told the Captain, what you do with your love life is your own concern."—Again, turning back to the ex-Sweeper—"So, how where they?" she said, with a wink.

Aware that she was being stared at by Killtooth, she remarked, "I was sore for days."—she smiled—"I just don't remember any of it," she giggled.

"That is a shame," Duplex replied, smiling and sensing she put Sweeper at ease.

"My Lord,"—Killtooth stepped up—"this way please, must not delay." They all proceeded to the meeting table. Everyone sat around the table except for Duplex, while Killtooth provided extra seating for Bollinger's night watch crew.

"Well, here we are," Duplex started to say. "You all know the situation, we are once again at war. We have found out that the Rear Guard of Rriban is alive and have been struggling to survive, but survive, they did. The evidence is sitting right there."—she pointed to Sarah who gave nervous smile—"We are going to be the spearhead of the liberation, however, we are going to deal with the traitor that is helping them, which is the reason for the cloak and dagger."

"I'm not a traitor!" the former Sweeper protested, with everyone staring at her.

"I know you not," Duplex said, and everyone looked at her with shock and surprise in their faces. "I knew for sure, soon as I arrived here. I knew when Captain Tyrik called me; I knew when the traitor arrived and made a mistake at the fleet... Lord Thant."

"What? How?" Killtooth exclaimed, as the amazement continued.

"Lord Thant was a guest of Intelligence during the civil war. As part of the lock down procedure, he learned the layout of Intelligence. He was reported going to the data core and accessed one of the terminals; all information was wiped.

"We also checked Sweeper's account. The same amount of money that was transferred into Cryptic M's former Sweeper's bank account was transferred into this sweeper's account after Dark Knight Biaci and I landed planet side.

"The only person who knew where we were going, was myself, my former apprentice Fidus, Lord Thant and our Emperor.

"My former apprentice is dead; the Emperor is beyond question. The only one who remained in question was Lord Thant, however, we had no proof. We had whom we assumed was the traitor because there was evidence pointing to you. So, we had you watched and you, thankfully, found the Captain Tyrik, who is a friend of mine." She winked at the ex-Sweeper.

"So you are the mutual friend? You lied to me," Ex-sweeper remarked, looking at Killtooth.

"I'm sorry, I had to keep you off track," he replied.

"So who else is here that made the ship go faster?" she asked again, looking at both Killtooth and Duplex.

"The Emperor," Bellis spoke clearly, as he stood up. "You replied 'three one three' in Morse code."

"Right," Duplex said, smiling. "We are returning to Rriban; our Emperor needs to make his presence known."

Duplex turned to the ex-Sweeper. "I understand you were never given a name. This is becoming a problem, as we cannot keep calling you Reader Eight and we cannot just keep calling you Ex-Sweeper."—Duplex started to pace the floor—"Let's see, you were an Agent of the Republic, turned informant, gained the trust of Cryptic M, awarded a Reader Eight position, trained my partner, Biaci, when she was Reader Six. You took over the Intelligence during the fight for Kaas City. You've sacrificed both of the men you cared for deeply, Cryptic M and my former apprentice. You've carried around with you the pain, the hurt, the frustrations that come with the position of Sweeper; that one night of freedom perhaps was your cry for help. I had no idea you were so close to Fidus. You may be interested to know that Sarah here"—she paused to wave at Sarah, directing her to come over—"You looked after Biaci like she was your own sister, you loved JB700 like your own brother. Sarah, is JB700's and Biaci's sister."

The ex-Sweeper's head snapped up, fully alert. By now, the flood gates were wide open as tears streamed down her face. Duplex knew Cryptic M was a sensitive subject for those around that time, however, everything Duplex mentioned hit the nail right on the head.

"Also Sarah, the ex-sweeper here took on a Dark Royal Guard and a Dark Knight in bed, and conquered them both."

Sarah came up close to the ex-Sweeper and hugged her tight. She had never met the woman before, but she could clearly see by how much emotion she was expressing, she was in pain from just the mention of her brother's and sister's names.

"Sarah," Duplex continued, "I have been granted the authority to perform and finalize the adoption ceremony. You, as the leading and only representative of your family, would you sponsor her into your family to become a sister?"

"I would be proud to have her as a sister. Does this mean we have to share boys now?" Sarah said sarcastically.

"However, we arrive at the problem again; the adoption needs you to have a name." Duplex waved her hands up in the air and back down. "Well, I guess that does it. There is no other option. You will just have to become a Dark Knight."

This put the ex-Sweeper in all out shock and disbelief. As she was frozen in place, Sarah put an arm around her. Nodding frantically, as she was unable to speak, she pointed to herself as if asking, did she really mean me?

"You've more than earned it. You didn't originate from Rriban or Kaas City; you don't entirely agree with all our methods, however, you stick to your duty and even when you hated your job, you still did it. Despite your own personal feelings, you still performed. You have all those pent-up emotions, that pain, hurt, anger, and love. You were already descendant from the White Knight, so you already knew you had the power inside of you. Kneel before me and swear your loyalty to me," Duplex Agens demanded.

Slowly, she got to one knee, and spoke the words, "I swear to serve, honor, and obey you, to become the best Dark Knight, to be able to destroy everyone who stands in my way."

"Who you once were, you are no more. Your past dies with you joining the family of Fidus, Biaci, and Sarah. Your past dies with the suffering of being wrongly accused of treason. Rise, Duplex Edge."—Duplex Agens turned—"I will now perform the adoption."

"HALT!" the slow creepy voice of the Emperor echoed. The door opened and four Dark Royal Guards entered. The room suddenly became bitterly cold as the Emperor followed his guards, entering the room.

"I hereby revoke my Saber's authority to perform the ceremony." He walked up slowly as everyone bowed, including Duplex Agens and Duplex Edge.

"Duplex Edge, stand before me," the Emperor's almost silent voice commanded. "Did you announce to anyone the Apprenticeship of Duplex Agens and Biaci?"

"No, my Emperor, I obeyed your orders," replied Duplex Edge, half shaking.

"Good." The Emperor turned and the black fog formed a huge display. Tiny little pictures appeared, showing the Dark Council, excluding Lord Thant, and the Admirals of every outpost or station, and the radio signal response even from Rriban. Duplex Agens recognized most of the images.

"The Dark Empire is about to reclaim what is ours. To Rriban, I am coming, you are not forgotten. For now, I hereby declare my Saber's new apprentice is Duplex Edge. The former Apprentice was killed; my Saber's Apprentice here forth is Duplex Edge.

"Duplex Edge, Saber, and Sarah, please stand next to me." All three of them stood, while a large bowl formed out of the fog.

"Dark Knight Master Duplex Agens, do you give your consent for your Apprentice Duplex Edge to enter into an existing Dark Knight family line?"

"I give consent," Duplex Agens replied.

"Sarah, as the leading representative of your family, with your Sister listening as a witness, do you accept Duplex Edge into your family line?"

"I give consent," Sarah stated.

"Duplex Edge and Sarah, with palms open, place your hands over the bowl. Sarah, place your hand above." They did so, and the Dark fog formed into a knife. Moving upwards, it sliced open the palm of Duplex Edge's hand, letting blood drip into the bowl. The knife proceeded up and cut into Sarah's hand.

The blood from Sarah's hand fell down onto Duplex Edge's open wound and the two different types of blood joined as they fell into the bowl.

"You blood has been joined. Duplex Edge, force the hand of Sarah, your sister, into the bowl to complete the process." As she did, blue flames surrounded their hands and arms. Their first reaction was to pull back, though the fog and fire kept their hands in place.

"It is done; the two separate lines have become one. The power of the Dark side has been strengthened. The bloodline of a descendant of the White Knights has joined with the Dark Knights, forever empowering us while weakening them. Power to the Empire." The symbol showed up and the signal was over.

"It is time we were on our way; the war and blood is waiting for us," Emperor stated, sounding eager. Finally everyone cheered along with the Emperor.

# CHAPTER 14.2

"Master, does this mean the Emperor is coming here?" Fortis asked. They had all been listening around the radio, Biaci, Captains Jack, David, and Jarad, along with all the original two hundred members of the Rear Guard.

"As I said during the initial meeting, the Emperor has never forgotten your suffering and you've just heard your proof. He spoke personally to you all." Biaci stood up and turned as she announced to everyone that had surrounded to listen to the broadcast. "The final combat is drawing near. Everyone that does not have a weapon, any children and wounded, take them to the basement at my old home. We converted it into a shelter in the last conflict."

"My Lord," Captain David spoke. He waited for Biaci to nod permission to continue speaking. "As is custom, we all extend to you our congratulations for your family growing."

"Thank you, Captain. What is the status of our forces? What kind of strength can we expect to put up now we've been reinforced?" Biaci demanded, looking across at all of the Captains.

"Out of the personnel belonging to the Rear Guard, we have now eight thousand armed with adequate weapons. We have forty eight Dark Military from Captain Jarad's crew," Captain Jack reported.

"We have two gun turrets, converted one missile launcher into anti-air defense. The second missile turret is setup on your lookout building for anti-armor defense. All weapons are set to use the ammunition standard for the scout ship. We have standard regulation ammunition for when the charge packs run out. We've resupplied the two tanks you've captured, thankfully they accept normal standard ammunition," reported Jarad.

"Remember to instruct the people under your commands to fire only at the power users whose area already engaged with either Master Biaci or her Apprentice," Captain David said aloud. "My Lord, do you have any idea how long it will take for them to get here?"

"Do not get your hopes up; it is better to assume no help is coming at all than to rely on someone else. They will have their own assigned mission to target the explosives or the person with the code to set them off. The Emperor's presence will simply be symbolic. "

It was getting late, the sun was just at the horizon now; it would be pitch dark soon. Biaci had everyone who was in the meeting held by her sister, her master Duplex Agens, and herself. Biaci had heard the Emperor's message. Having declared her master's new apprentice, this cemented the fact that Biaci and her master had to fight. It was good, staying still for too long blunts your weapon's edge. However, that was not the reason she wanted to fight. Biaci had believed her master was carrying her brother's baby and was manipulated into protecting Duplex Agens. She had played on Biaci's need and want for a family to use her to kill her own brother.

With the knowledge of them coming to the planet, it brought all of this back to the surface and it made Biaci feel more like her old self. She enjoyed risks and calculated gambles, and she had one in mind.

The situation for the Rear Guard of Rriban looked grim. Biaci, agreeing with her Apprentice, had assumed they were going to hit with their strongest punch, which would be their power users. However, they swapped the placement of the armored units with their front line ground troops, so the armored units faced the enemy; it left their armored units incredibly exposed. The ground troops behind could not see anything ahead of them because of the units.

There were sixteen armored units, split into two pairs of eight, separated by the road which lead to the Intelligence building.

"Gentleman, we need to discuss what I have planned for tonight. As it is close to getting dark, it will be time soon. At their perimeter of the no-man's area, they have their armored units, which threaten artillery fire. This will be a chance to wipe their confidence from them. They believe they are safe, over there thinking we don't dare come out. When this works, we will change all of that."

Biaci walked back over to the head table and requested, "Apprentice, please explain one more time, the steps."

Fortis stood up and cleared her throat. "The plan is simple, a simple magician act. Captain Jarad and Captain David will go out into the middle under a flag of truce. Once we have confirmed with them we want to talk, Captains Jarad and David will keep them busy. As further distraction, we will have the guns and armored units rotate their guns and start the engines to create noise. My master taking the right flank and myself taking the left flank, using the speed ability, we will make it over to their outer most armored units, place the charges, and withdraw back to our lines. We only need to set one off on each side; with them being so close, they will cascade and set them all off. Show the Republic, we can hit out."

"Dark Knight Fortis, what are we to talk about that will keep them out there for that long?" Captain Jack asked. Fortis looked to Biaci for an answer.

"You will give them the chance to surrender; you will explain exactly this,"—she stood up—"meaning you may want to write it down, so you don't forget." Biaci paced the floor waiting for the Captains to recover their notebooks.

"The Rear Guard of Rriban is giving you your way out, with no lives having to die pointlessly. Our Emperor is coming and will be on land by the day's end, followed by the fleet. You could attempt kill us now for nothing and just be slaughtered. Dark Knight Master Biaci permits us to offer you two possible options.  One, you sign a non-aggression agreement and we allow every Republic soldier to leave unharmed, the planet for the Republic is lost.  Option two, you surrender to us and no harm will come to you, and you will be treated fairly.  How you want to lose is up to you. One of you, go speak to your General, one stay here."

"You are, of course, missing the huge potential hole in the plan; the crew of the armored units, you expect them to not be able to see you?" questioned Captain Jarad.

"I have seen my Master while she has done this; while using her speed she is a blur, you blink, you miss her. At night, she will be impossible to see," Fortis answered.

"Yes, she left me for dust as she ran to the tallest building. As Fortis said, you blink, you miss her," Captain David added.

"That is nice and all, but you will not be a blur when you stop to place the charges. You need to plan for failure, so you would need to place a charge on at least two armored units in case of failure," Captain Jarad replied.

"What happens on the off chance they accept our terms?" Captain Jack asked.

"We carry out the Emperor's orders, no prisoners. If they choose to leave, we let them. However, I don't believe this will become a reality," Biaci explained. "Also, Captain Jarad, once we are up close enough, they will not be able to see us; we can squat down and our robes gives us perfect camouflage. I am not going to try to persuade you there is no risk because I do acknowledge there is."

"Which is exactly why you are doing this... Apprentice," said a mysterious voice. Then the barn door busted open with Duplex Agens and Duplex Edge appearing at the entrance. They entered slowly as everyone looked stunned. They just heard them on the radio, and now they were here?

"Is our Emperor with you?" asked Biaci.

"He is on the ship still and he..." she started to say, answering the unspoken question, "is why we are here so fast. Dark Knight Master Biaci, allow me to introduce—"

"Sweeper?!" Biaci interrupted, stunned by the appearance.

"No, I am Duplex Edge, and officially your sister now." Duplex Edge was beaming from ear to ear as she hugged Biaci. Nothing would have stopped her.

"Apprentice... Sorry. My new Apprentice, back off. They have a task to do."—Duplex Agens turned, smiling at Fortis—"We can get reacquainted after they are done. I hope you will honor our agreement to not fight until after we are done here?" Agens finished, directing her question to Biaci, even though she had not stopped looking at Fortis.

She walked up to Fortis and put a hand on her shoulder. Until then Fortis had only had her master's powers to borrow, but had heard of Biaci's master's power of Dark Power manipulation. As soon as she saw Duplex Agens, she began trying to borrow her power of manipulation and use it against her.

"Dark Power syphon is incredibly useful, however, it has limits, such as you can only borrow one power. Someone who has manipulation can shield their mind from attacks. That, if any power, should be the one you borrow from me. However, I can see you've come a long way, Fortis," she said, smiling.

"How did you know I borrowed it?" asked Fortis.

"The second limitation. Just because you are borrowing it does not mean the person you are borrowing it from cannot use it at the same time." Duplex paused, as she started to talk inside Fortis' mind.

"Also, when you enter the mind, if you have a wall up, you can feel someone trying to enter, like knocking on the door. You have no wall, so soon as I felt you trying to enter mine, I looked inside of yours, and learned you were just being curious, which was why I didn't strike," Duplex Agens stated, while tapping Fortis' shoulder. "You've chosen well, Biaci. She is very strong and isn't afraid, even of me. It is good to see you, but now, go do whatever crazy thing you are planning to do."

~

"What is the status? Are we ready to move out?" General Chester asked Sergio.

"The process will be completed soon. It is taking longer due to being down two shuttles, which suffered malfunctions after their initial trips. The pilots attempted to take more people back up than they should and it overloaded stabilizers," reported Sergio.

"So how much has that set us back by?" replied Chester.

"One hour, General." Anticipating Chester's next response Sergio continued, "It would normally take two, however, given the seriousness, we are going to get it done in one hour."

"Make sure you leave a security detail on your ship; it is going to be a tempting target. They've got communications now; they would of told their fleet. We have to assume they have designs to stop the ship leaving," remarked Chester, before he turned to leave.

It was late and the two men were outside. While Chester was walking along the lines checking on his men, giving surprise hellos and asking how they were doing. Chester saw sometimes it did good for morale, it lets the men know they are not forgotten. However, he made sure he stayed clear of the superstitious, believing it to be bad luck if their commanding officer came to speak to them before a battle. Chester never really believed in it too much, but he knew they did and it would be them that fought this battle, not him. The sun was finally hidden beneath the horizon revealing a clear night sky, though there was no moon in sight.

"General Chester, sir," said a voice from the shadows, as Chester walked by the entrance to the HQ on his way to inspect the other side.

"Yes?" Chester responded with a short answer. Then a person five foot eight inches high emerged from the darkness, carrying two glasses.

"General Chester, sir,"—Rockwell stepped out—"If you permit it, I wanted one last drink with you. Normally I would toast before a battle with my son..." Rockwell paused and looked down for a moment. Chester did not say anything out of respect and waited for Rockwell to pull himself back together. "I will not be able to do it tomorrow as I will be..."

Now Chester interrupted, "It will be a pleasure." He took one of the glasses. "What do you toast to?"

"To going home, normally," Rockwell said, drifting off at the end.

Chester, not missing a beat, raised his glass and announced, "TO GOING HOME!" Rockwell did the same and the two gentleman tapped their glasses before downing the glasses of brandy.

"Thank you, sir. Now to one item of business. I realized the mistake we made before by planning everything on one plan, and we are doing the same again, putting everything on Sergio coming through for us. I have come up with a little back-up to make sure someone gets out to let someone back home know what is going on here. I want to keep it just between you and I and the person involved. Would you mind following me, sir? I have the person already waiting in the briefing room."

Chester nodded, while he started to follow. Then a white burst flare launched from the Non-Republic side, getting everyone's attention.

"Is it an attack?" General Chester shouted.

"Sir, they are communicating," the Republic signalman trooper reported. "Sir, they want to talk in person. They intend to send two people out in the middle to talk, and request we send two people, no weapons. Response?"

"Ask them, just to talk?" Rockwell insisted.

The Republic trooper sent the series of flashes and waited for the response, "Yes sir, just to talk."

"Commander Rockwell, have Commanders William and Thomas report to me on the double," General Chester ordered.

Rockwell ran off as he said, "Trooper, tell them we require ten minutes."

Again, the series of flashes were sent with another series of flashes received, "We have four minutes, sir."

"Sir, we are here," the Commanders said from behind Chester, all sounding out of breath. "Instructions?"

"Just don't give the game away. Go out and see what they want," the General ordered.

"Commander Douglas!" the General shouted. "Commander Douglas!" he shouted again, but Douglas still did not come.

"General, sir, Douglas is on duty assigned by me. I brought you your glasses." Rockwell handed Chester his glasses, and as he put the strap over his head, he looked towards Rockwell and asked, "What is the duty you assigned to him?"

"Not here, General, and not now. We were interrupted as I was going to explain, so for now, I guess we just have to wait and see what they want. Any idea what they want?" Rockwell was deflecting and Chester knew it because of the fact he declined to respond and just proceeded half way down the road to the edge of the no-man's land.

"Their representatives have started to come out, sir," Rockwell reported. "Their Dark Knight handed something to them. Strange she has her hood up. Permission to call out the guard? Just as precaution, sir, given what happened last time we had a ceasefire."

Chester nodded yes in response.

"To arms! Trooper, sound the alert!" Rockwell bellowed. The sound of a drum being beaten with the skin vibrating began to penetrate the air. At the same time, the noise of tanks and guns warming up came across the barren lands of no man's land, where the four men now stood in the middle.

"Hopefully this is just Saber rattling, otherwise this will rather screw up our plans, Commander."—Chester turned to face Rockwell—"General, whatever it is you have set up, do not wait to tell me or to seek approval. Go do whatever it is; the less people know, including me, the better." Chester saluted and Rockwell saluted in return before disappearing into HQ.

Chester stood there alone, as only General's could when standing surrounded by companies and lines of infantry. However, right now, standing in this spot, he felt like the loneliest person around, since all he could do was wait, and the responsibility for everything and everyone rested squarely on his shoulders.

He raised his glasses looking out to the wasteland. Commander Thomas turned and headed back with a very serious look on his face, whereas William stayed with the two men. It seemed like forever until Thomas reached their lines, despite him running.

"Well, what is it Commander?" General Chester demanded.

"Sir, you may want to do this in more discrete matter," Thomas offered, with a pleading look on his face.

"Out with it. They are waiting for the response and I'm not going to dilly-dally about it."—he gave Thomas a serious look—"Now, Commander, with the Bark on."

"Sir, they state the planet for the Republic is lost; the Emperor is coming and may even be planet side already. They stated by day's end; I believe this was a lie. They give us two choices, sign an agreement and we can all leave with our lives, or surrender to them and they assure us no harm will come to us, like the cooks and other staff members that defected and decided to sit out the conflict instead of fighting for either side. They state the planet is lost, no point throwing away lives for nothing. It is our choice how we want to lose." Anxiety covered Commander Thomas's face as he recited their demands.

General Chester opened his mouth to speak, however, instead of his voice being heard, a trip mine explosion went off and immediately illuminated flares were fired into the air at Chester's far left.

"Report!" the General shouted, as a small company went to investigate.

"All clear! Looks like an accidental detonation, no bodies or limbs in sight, sir. No signs of any enemy activity," they reported.

"Commander," Chester said, turning back to Thomas. "Pass my respects; make sure you say thank you for your offer, however, we must reject. It is do or die from here on out," Chester said and saluted.

Commander Thomas didn't wait, he had already double timed back out. Looking through his glasses, Chester saw his man reach his destination. The non-Republic Captain's faces turned to grim expressions, but neither looked surprised. They saluted and he saw the captain he was familiar with, Captain David, shake hands and handed something to William. Then the four men parted, and once again, the two commanders returned back to their lines.

"Stand down from alert, trooper," shouted General Chester. Once again, the drum beat with the skin vibrating the stand-down signal.

"General, sir," William saluted. "Captain David stated to say, sir, he totally understands. He personally would of made the same decision, however, their offer had to be made. He also passed this to me from his masters to you." William handed over a wrapped bundle.

Chester took the bundle and cut the binding with his knife, letting the wrapping fall away, leaving only a circle medallion in his palm.

"Is that the Caborn medallion from the Emperor's Saber?" William asked.

"No, Commander, it is gold, the gold medallion of the Emperor. He has marked me for death personally," Chester said, almost silently. He turned to walk away, but no sooner than he turned, all three men were lifted off their feet and landed, face first, four feet away from where they had originally been standing. The force and heat of the explosions of their armored units started going up in flames. All units except for two on the left side had gone up in flames. Commander William lifted his head up, still dazed. He looked over at General Chester; his back looked burnt with his clothes all torn and smoking, not moving. William turned his head only to the right and saw Commander Thomas, standing behind both of them. He had shielded them from most of the blast. His back was on fire, but thankfully he would not feel any of that pain, as William noticed a piece of armored plating sticking out Thomas' back.

"Commander, Commander! You ok?" William heard someone say. He couldn't tell who; he just smelled something funny. He looked round and saw his back was smoking. That was when the pain hit him, and mercifully, he passed out.

# CHAPTER 16

Admiral Soemu was on watch at the bridge of the Morgan Rice, sitting in the command chair that commanded the bridge, with the view of the dark space around the ship.

The bridge was silent except for the sounds of the terminals and the computer responses. The tension in the room was thick; no one said anything. One of the ship's ensigns reported to his commanding officer by presenting the pad needing his authorization in complete silence.

On the ceiling, the ship's time device had been counting down the forty eight hours set by the Emperor's Saber. The tension was coming from knowing that soon, the fleet, after days of waiting around, would finally move out to the planet of Rriban to liberate the planet and take it from the hands of the enemy to reclaim their homes.

The instructions had been given, that everyone was to be armed. The ship was put on a war footing. The military should never be without their weapons, including the navy as well. A blaster was propped up against the admiral's chair. It had been a while since he had the chance to use a weapon; he relished the feeling, he felt young again. This was the worst part, the waiting, not knowing what was happening on Rriban. The feeling was echoed throughout his crew. Some felt a conflict; many had come to call Kaas City their home, however, Rriban never stopped being the home of the Dark Knights or the Dark Empire.

"You have lust for battle, Admiral?" Thant asked from behind.

White Knight, dammit, Soemu thought to himself. He had not heard him come in, but he quickly stood and bowed. "Sorry, my Lord."

Lord Thant took the chance now; he stood and raised his hand to suggest he didn't have to rush an empty gesture. "You've done well, Admiral. The blood lust your crew is expressing is very strong; they're hungry for battle, as they should be."

"My Lord?" Soemu responded, unsure of what he was supposed to say.

"I understand you have been given authority over me, is this correct?"

Thant's voice became cold.

Admiral Soemu did not need to be a Dark Knight to know this conversation was dangerous. He tactfully chose what to say. "Only in military situations, my Lord, and items of that nature."

"Admiral, I want to send a scout ship ahead to provide us feedback of what is going on planet side. Just purely observation, it is too dangerous not knowing what is going on between now and when we go. Our Emperor is en route; as Admiral, you should ensure his safety." Lord Thant said, playing on the crew's feelings. Even the Admiral wanted to know what was happening.

"What kind of scout ship?" Admiral Soemu questioned, still unsure.

"We have heard nothing from that observation scout ship; we have to assume they have been compromised. I have assigned the crew and they're ready to set off, given your authorization, of course," Lord Thant stated, having to force a calm tone in his voice. He'd like nothing more than to take what he wanted.

"I should check this with Admiral Takeo," Soemu decided, still uncertain.

"Are you going to need Admiral Takeo to hold your hand when you are fighting for our home?" That did it, Lord Thant knew instantly.

Admiral Soemu went over to the arm of the chair and pressed the communicator, "Authorization granted, my Lord. I will report this to Dragomire."

Lord Thant turned and vowed to himself, he would not beg again next time, soon, but not yet. He had just reached the exit of the bridge when it opened and Sarah stepped through the door.

"My Lord,"—she bowed—"I was coming to see you."

"Well, you have seen me, now remove yourself from my sight." Lord Thant's patience expired, having vented it all on Admiral Soemu. He was not in a mood to entertain the plaything of the Emperor's Saber.

"My Lord, please don't judge me too harshly. I know yourself and the

Emperor's Saber have a strained relationship; I assure you our companionship was that of necessity for the Empire, not pleasure. My Lord, I can assure you my sincerity." Sarah handed over a very small bundle.

Lord Thant took it and had started to opened it, but Sarah interrupted. "Not here, my Lord!" she said quickly. "In here." Sarah pointed to the lift as the door closed and she sealed the door.

The wrapping fell off revealing the picture frame holding the picture of Fidus with the name tag, "Sweeper."

"What is the meaning of this? Tell me now or you will not live long enough to see your home world again," Lord Thant snarled.

"My Lord, I was ordered to fly a ship to a spot in space. The Saber met up with Dark Knight Killtooth and the former Sweeper, the traitor. The Saber has made the former Sweeper, the traitor, her new Apprentice. That is my proof that I was there. She was very fond of Dark Knight Fidus, and that is her Sweeper tag," she said, almost confidently.

"You bring this as your proof? Proof of what? That the Emperor's Saber is a coconspirator?" Lord Thant had not survived this long to trust at random.

"The Saber rescued me off the planet to which I was trapped for almost a decade; I felt loyal to her for that. However, I have never betrayed the Empire. I never joined the Republic; I stayed loyal to the end, my Lord. It is my proof of my loyalty to the Empire, to the Dark Council, which you are a representative of." She got down on her knees and bowed.

Lord Thant saw no deception as he used the Dark Power to penetrate Sarah's mind; he saw she did pilot the ship she spoke of, and saw Sweeper and the extra people.

"Why were the crew of the Dragomire with the Saber?" he asked.

"I was not informed they were part of a mission headed by the Saber. All I was told was to fly them there and come back, my Lord," she whimpered.

Again, he looked further into her mind and saw she told the truth. He attempted to go further, however, all he saw was black.

"You have done well. Return to the Dragomire; when I need you, I will call for you. Your loyalty to the Empire is noted. Now LEAVE," he commanded.

Sarah did not hesitate. She got up, opened the lift doors, and left as Thant headed back down. Lord Thant opened up a mini halo communicator.

"I've secured you a ship, as requested. They will be at the assigned coordinates you specified within the next two hours. Imperial markings have been removed." He ended the call and looked at the picture in the frame.

"You were full of potential, Fidus," he said to himself, as the lift doors opened and he proceeded to the guest room that was assigned to him. The doors opened. "Your death was a waste, however, if Biaci hadn't killed you when she did, I would have had to deal with you." He set the picture aside on the desk as he entered the room. "It was easy to stall Cryptic M; I doubt you would have been so easy, given you were an Apprentice, not a Cryptic agent," he sighed.

He walked over to the side table, which had a mini terminal he brought with him. It had access to the Dark Empire Database, a direct link. He was able to make unmonitored communications using a remote connection through this device with a virtual protocol network. It allowed him, although being lightyears away from Kaas City, to connect to the network used on Kaas, as if he was there himself.

He looked at the time display, and pressed the power button to the terminal as he sat down. Then he set the terminal to receive mode and waited. He was not used to being kept waiting; he was a Lord of the Dark Council, people did as he ordered.

There was a low hum emanating from the lights of the room. It annoyed Lord Thant almost to the point of distraction, when the light on the transmission indicator suddenly started flashing a blue light. The flag of the Republic was displayed across the screen for a split second before the screen changed to the image of General Rockwell.

"I do not appreciate you keeping me waiting, General. Need I remind you what is at stake here. I am the last grip the Republic has inside of the

Dark Council." Lord Thant was disgruntled; he did not care why Rockwell looked disheveled and dirty.

"Your friends," Rockwell said, putting emphasis on the last word, "they've just killed General Chester; I am the only active commander in charge. The next in command is Master Sergio, and you heard his delight when he learned I was working with you," General Rockwell said, agitated.

"Explain, now!" Lord Thant demanded, his anger venting.

"They held a truce, so they could talk; they offered a chance to surrender. General Chester received the Gold medallion of the black hand." Rockwell waited to see if this sparked a response from Lord Thant, it did. Rockwell started running out of air, as Lord Thant had started closing the air around Rockwell's throat.

"You mean to tell me, the Emperor is already on Rriban?" Lord Thant raised his hand and vented his anger toward that annoying buzzing light, causing it to shatter from the pressure of Lord Thant's Dark Power.

"The ship should already be in system; have your men ready. We cannot have any more surprises. Although, the presence of the Emperor may work in our favor. I am your official next in command, you know what that means?" ordered Lord Thant, as he let go of the pressure around Rockwell's throat

"How are you going to do your part?" Rockwell demanded.

"That is not your concern. Just do your job and transmit what is needed. If you fail again, I will complete what you failed to do. If this goes well, I will be in control of the Empire." Lord Thant smiled as he shut off the terminal and left the file transfer protocol running.

Now Thant just had to figure out how he was going to do his part. He had to delay the dreadnaughts now. The engine shut down had been removed, an unfortunate mistake, as he realized this meant the Emperor's Saber, and in turn the Emperor, would have been suspicious, if they didn't already know.

He opened the communicator he had used earlier. "Sarah, your time to serve me is at hand." He did not know if he could take her at her word. He looked at the picture of Fidus; he had no choice, even he, powerful as he was, could not be in two places at once.

"These are your orders…" he said, as he started to explain to Sarah.

# CHAPTER 17

"It is done, my Emperor." The Emperor's Saber was back aboard the ship orbiting Rriban. "I've made sure their current General receives your mark."

"You have... figured out... what I intend to do?" the Emperor drawled in a slow creepy voice. The observation level had been transformed into a replica of the Emperor's thrown room; the Dark Power fog had taken over everything. Only seeing, only allowing what the Emperor wanted. No one outside or on the level below could get in or overhear what was happening. The Dark Royal guards had been positioned below to ensure this fact, since everyone left to complete their missions.

"Not entirely, my Emperor. I'm unclear how you intend to play this," Duplex Agens replied. "We have to be very careful with this. I understand the sacrifice that needs to be made, however, if anyone ever found out, I think we would have a full scale revolt."

"Did your friend make it back to the fleet on time?" asked the Emperor.

"She reported contact and he has the gift, my Emperor," Duplex reported.

"Good..." he said with a grin, "Needed to be punished."

"I do not understand, how does giving him a gift punish him?" she inquired with a puzzled look over her face. The Emperor did not get to respond, as a signal flashed through the Dark Power fog, which receded to reveal the control panel wall.

"Your Apprentice, Dark Knight Biaci, has succeeded. An explosion was just monitored from the ground," reported the Emperor. "You are dismissed. Return and commence part two. Tell the night watch to start."

~

Lt. Bollinger looked at the inside of his wrist, which held the time device provided to him for the task. He looked towards Waller and asked, "Did you make the incision yet?" His voice was muffled because of the breather mask he was wearing.

"Just waiting for the go ahead, just as long as you know, if anyone is on the inside, they will hear us enter," Waller replied.

"Relax, the Dark Knight is already on the inside. I'm sure he has taken care of his part." Bollinger looked again at the time device on his right arm. He felt the left arm vibrate through his suit. He looked at it and saw the bright highlighted word, GO.

"NOW!" ordered Bollinger. Waller pressed the button on the device that was attached to the part of the hull, he had cut. It fired metal rods in all directions over the area Waller had cut, sealed it-self, and then with a small charge, pushed the metal hull fragment inside.

Waller floated backwards as he allowed Cody, Cole, and Jason inside; Bollinger approached and signaled Waller to go in ahead of him. Bollinger looked around, which was pointless as they were floating in space. It wasn't like there was anyone that would be in a position to spot them. However, his training was so embedded in him, he did it out of habit. He noticed how something as deadly as space was also very romantically beautiful.

As soon as he floated in, Waller came back up and replaced the metal fragment, which still had the device attached, repairing the hole through which they just entered.

"Hurry up, ten minutes remaining," Bollinger ordered.

Cody came up with a torch and started to weld the metal sheet in place. Waller with a second torch started to weld another side.

"Two minutes," Bollinger stated.

"You think that helps?" Cody was getting annoyed. Apparently, the pressure of time was getting to him.

At the same exact point when the time on Bollinger's time device clicked from one to zero, the lights came back on, illuminating the room. Waller and Cody just finished the very last section of the metal plate on their respective sides.

The ship's automated voice announced, "Power failure has been restored. Sections twenty one B, forty six A. Power has been restored." No alarms sounded, and there was no automatic detection of a hull breach.

"Great work guys." Bollinger patted each of their backs. They started taking their space gear off as the door opened.

"You guys made it then?" Killtooth inquired as he stepped through the door. Bollinger saw the body he was dragging behind him as he pulled him into the room. "This is going to be a lot easier than I thought; they've must of sent their entire crew down to the planet. There is almost no Knights aboard, just one in the engineering section," he remarked. "You guys ready? Any word from the other team?"

"None," said Bollinger. He looked around, and saw they had gotten their weapons strapped across their chests. Waller was carrying the backpack of tools they brought with them.

"Okay, follow me. Stay close; do exactly what I say. I've destabilized the adjoining section. No one will be able to come into this section for hours; they're not even trying to fix the problem. I set up a lot of distractions, so hopefully we will have a clear path to the jump drive," Killtooth explained.

~

Sarah, aboard the Dragomire, was taking the elevator down to Engineering. On the way down she felt the time device on her right wrist vibrate and knew it meant that Team One was already on their way. She needed to hurry and get to Morecambe. It would be the first time she saw him again since… since he helped relieve her of her frustrations. She liked him enough; he was cute. She just didn't have a lot of time at that particular moment, so she decided to skip a few steps and took what she wanted. She knew enough men in her life that wanted to do the exact same to her.

The doors opened and she ran out carrying rolled up maps and papers under her arm. She ran into the section and saw the other members of Morecambe's Engineering crew. They all had smirks on their faces. They know, she thought to herself, of course they know. He probably told all his friends. She didn't doubt, she was the best thing that had happened to him. Finally she saw him, leaning over working on a coupling that had come loose.

"Hmm, now that is a firm ass," she said to herself. "White Knight wept, get ahold of yourself, girl. Lives depend on you." She focused on her task.

"Morecambe!" she shouted, slightly louder than she intended. He looked up startled. "You got somewhere we can go private?" He started to smile again and Sarah knew what he was thinking. The bulge in his pants had started to grow. "No, Morecambe, this is business. Do you have anyone that knows Dreadnaughts like the one we encountered?"

Morecambe looked puzzled, but answered, "Yes."

"Let's go then. Morecambe, have your person join us on the double. This is urgent." Sarah growing increasingly frustrated, "MOVE, it's urgent."

Morecambe placed two fingers in his mouth and blew a sharp whistle. A man covered in grease from head to toe looked up. Morecambe did a circular movement above his head with his hand and the guy dropped everything.

"Let's go," he said, looking at Sarah, and they ran off toward the control room. "I take it you need a desk of some kind, judging by what's under your arm. My control room for damage control is perfect, and I can seal the doors, if you prefer."

Sarah nodded. "You have a halo-communicator device in there?"

"Not working," Morecambe replied.

"Damn, my hand device will have to do then." Sarah sped through the door ,almost knocking Morecambe over as she charged to the table and started unrolling the maps on the desk, placing a wrench on one corner.

Morecambe waited for his man to enter, then shut and sealed the door behind him. "This is sensitive information. Can you black out the windows?"

"Anyone would think you were planning to assassinate the Chancellor the way you're going," said Morecambe, as the electronic heat shield lowered into place, normally intended to protect him from engine fire or reactor blasts.

"What is your name?" Sarah demanded.

The man wiped his face with the standard issue rag each member of Morecambe's crew had to get the grease off their face and hands. He wiped his mouth so he could speak clearly. Sgt. Nung stood five foot four with black hair, and had a scar across his face from his right eye down to his right cheek. Somehow, he retained what was known as a Chinese accent back on Earth. No one knew how or why he would have such an accent, as the Dark Empire had left Earth centuries ago. Nung was only in his thirties, but the dirt and grease made him look like he was seventy.

"Sgt. Nung. David Nung, sir," he said to Sarah.

"How well you know the engines of the ship we went up against earlier, Sergeant?"—Sarah gave him a serious look—"Would you be able to talk someone through a procedure?"

"Captain Sarah, what is going on? I've allowed you to come into my department, order me around and get me up here, as you requested. Least you can—" he attempted to demand.

"Shut-up!" she interrupted him angrily. Then she turned back to Nung. "Well?"

"I served for eighteen months aboard a ship like that before I defected, Captain. The engine is like ours, less advanced, however. I could walk through someone, but they need to know what they are seeing. We cannot walk someone that is not inclined to this sort of thing."

"These are maps of the engine parts to a White Knight Super Dreadnaught, the latest we have. We have, ah—" she was about to explain, when a communications came through her wrist comm.

"Claw one to Dark two, we are in position. Do you receive?" Killtooth reported, followed by a static noise.

"This is Dark two, we got you. With me is a friend who will walk you through the steps. Do you have someone that knows a wrench from a hammer?"

"This is Claw one. Confirmed, standing by for instructions," Killtooth replied.

"Sergeant, I know this is a shock, maybe even a surprise to you. We have a squad on that ship attempting to sabotage the jump drive. We don't want to destroy, just so it fails soon as they start to jump. We want to delay the inevitable, that someone on Coroscate won't know what happened until we have already rebuilt on Rriban."

Sarah took the comm-strap off her wrist. "Claw one, this is Dark two. We are ready."

Sgt. Nung started to sweat as he looked towards Morecambe, who was just overseeing everything. "Okay, where are you currently located?"

"Claw 1 here, we are in a huge area with four giant cylinders, look like boilers." Sgt. David moved the maps and pointed to one where Sarah could see.

"Claw one, go to your right, You will see a door marked ER1; go through that door, hang a left, head down the corridor until you get to the first entryway on your right," David finished, giving the instructions.

"Claw 1 here, understood," Killtooth reported.

"The jump drive is in that one; they devoted an entire section to it," Nung said to Sarah.

"Claw 1, as you enter, you will see a panel on the wall to your left. You need one man there. At the same time, there is an identical panel on the opposite wall that will need another man. Further down the hall is a third panel; again, you need one man there. Any changes need to be done at all three panels at the exact same time. Any deviations, it cancels out everything and makes you start from scratch again. It's an inbuilt safe guard."

"Acknowledged, Dark one," Killtooth reported.

"Okay, I'll explain what to do to you, and you relay it to the other people. Again, they must be synced with each other. Everyone needs to unscrew the wall panel," Sgt. Nung instructed, and waited.

"Okay, the first thing they need to do is eliminate the red wire; cut the top section first, then the bottom second, and remove the cable." Again, Nung waited for Killtooth to relay the instructions.

"Okay, that is the last of the easy stuff. We will begin now…"

# CHAPTER 18

"It is time. Form up." Both General Rockwell and Master Biaci issued the same order to their troops. The Dark Empire and the Rear Guard both formed up at the barricade. Biaci, Fortis and Duplex Edge were at the front of the Dark Empire troops. The White Knights formed up on the opposite side of the barricade, ten lines deep. Master Sergio and Ramon flanked General Rockwell at the front.

"Do we kill him?" Duplex Edge asked, rather eagerly.

"No, capture him. If he is separated, he cannot set off the charges. With General Chester gone, the next senior officer is standing behind him and they are somewhat harder to kill," Dark Knight Master Biaci answered.

"Master, you were right. I am starting to feel apprehension, as you mentioned before," Fortis commented.

Biaci didn't get to respond. As she was about to speak, Captain Jack replaced Captain David, and he returned to his gun battery position. Jack then began to sing,

> *"He's forty shillings on the drum,*
> *For those who volunteer to come,*
> *To 'list and fight the foe today,*
> *Over the hills and far away."*

Captain Jack looked at them all as they stared back at him. "It is a very old song. The main difference is we use our emotions when they deny it. They need to know what they are going up against." Biaci then gave him the nod to carry on with the song, much to Jack's surprise.

Captain Jack picked up where he left off after the first verse. After he finished the first part of the chorus, the rest of the Rear Guard joined in.

> *"When duty calls me I must go,*
> *To stand and face another foe,*
> *But part of me will always stray,*
> *Over the hills and far away."*

"I understand now, Master. The song is helping us focus. I feel stronger," Fortis said, looking up and smiling.

"What is it they are singing?" Master Sergio asked Rockwell.

"Over the hills and far away," replied Rockwell. "They are using their advantage. They have emotions; they are drawing their strength from it."

"They have misplaced their faith in the wrong place; it is the weapon with a clear mind that wins the fight," Master Sergio said.

"You couldn't be more wrong, things like honor and clear thought get left behind, soon as we take a step forward. The only thing you will feel should be quivering fear, the hope that you die a clean death and not an agonizing blow. The only way to win what is to come, is to lose yourself in the rage. Anything else, you will hold back when you need to step forward. Battle is the direct consequence of chaos, just as chaos is a direct consequence of battle. There is nothing calm, nothing civil about organized killing like this. Emotions can make you stronger than you can imagine," stated Rockwell.

"Like love?" Master Ramon remarked, speaking with a tone that was anything but sincere.

"Like love. As you can see there is three Dark Knights now, there is more about, I am sure. However, I've been informed Duplex Edge is the former Sweeper of Intelligence. She had no name before now because you people executed her parents before her mother could present her with a name. By your own actions, we created a potential deadly weapon for our enemy. She was a daughter of the White Knights and now she stands in front of us; do you think this is because she was told to?"

Rockwell tilted his head and sighed. He looked across the soon to be the battleground and caught the attention of Dark Knight Master Biaci. He saluted using the sword to place in front of his face, Biaci acknowledged the salute. The singing got louder and more intense from behind the barricade.

"Let the drums beat," Rockwell ordered. Once again the drums were beaten, the skins of the drums vibrated. It was as if the entire world, nature included, remained quiet while both sides competed against each other, the drums from the White Knights against the singing of the Rear

Guard.

"LOUDER," Biaci ordered. "You too, Apprentice Duplex Edge. Show them we are not afraid."

"Dun, boom, dun boom, boom boom, click click, dun boom, dun boom, boom, boom, boom." The sound of the drums rang out across the battle field.

"FORWARD!" Rockwell ordered.

The drums were answered with more singing.

> *"Faded away like the stars in the morning,*
> *Losing their light in the glorious sun—*
> *Thus would we pass from this earth and its toiling,*
> *Only remembered for what we have done."*

"To battle." The two forces marched forward, preparing to clash in the middle. The Rear Guard stopped after taking six paces forward, then knelt to present arms. The tanks fired four rounds of smoke shot wide across the land. As they crashed into the ground, the canisters broke, allowing smoke to billow out, masking the army coming ahead of Biaci. She looked up and saw escape pods coming from the sky, but forced herself to look ahead.

The White Knights, being led by General Rockwell, continued forward into the smoke cloud. Both Master Sergio and Ramon placed a hand on Rockwell's shoulder and allowed the troopers to walk past. refusing to let Rockwell walk into the trap.

The two remaining armored units moved forward to protect the flanks. At the same time, four shuttles, sent on a bombing run, flew over their heads. They had just gone beyond the smoke cloud and all they heard was four fast shots and what sounded like two missiles being fired. Then there were three rather loud crashes, and they saw the last shuttle flying over their heads as it had tried to make it back. It crashed into the buildings, including the old building that used to be Rockwell's headquarters before they moved him to the Intelligence building.

Masters Sergio, Ramon, and Rockwell all waited as they saw the men walk into the smoke clouds. The three fire sabers were ignited, followed by the sounds and images of the white fire of the blades of the White Knights. A missile was fired from a tall building, narrowly missing one of the tanks, while a shot was fired from one of the tanks behind the barricade, intended for the armored unit. However, it overshot the target and landed behind in the middle of the advancing White Knights, killing forty of them on the spot.

"CHARGE!" Rockwell ordered, and they started to run into the cloud now.

The three crimson fire sabers were waving and twirling around in the fog, as both fire and white fire blades burned away the smoke cloud.

"Tell your ship to go now." Rockwell had turned on the spot to face Sergio, who in turn raised his wrist communicator "This is Master Sergio, depart."

"Acknowledged, Master," the voice of his squire sounded.

Each of the three Dark Knights had at least four White Knights on them. Biaci used both of her blades as she parried one blow. They did not have to worry about getting in the way of their friends, whereas the White Knights, surrounded by allies, had to be careful where and when to strike, as they could have killed their friends before hitting one of the Dark Knights' sabers.

Those that started to push on through the smoke cloud were greeted by rapid fire barrage from the gun turrets aknd Rear Guard that held their ground, firing not directly at the White Knights, but at their feet. They knowing the White Knights would just reflect the shots if they aimed higher. This tactic was slowly pushing the White Knights back into the cloud to face the Dark Knights.

The other turrets, when clear, were aiming at the White Knights heavily engaged with Duplex Edge and Fortis, as per Biaci's orders.

"They are not as experienced as I am; they will need more protection than I," Biaci stated. Blasts sounded and dirt flew skywards as shots landed, missing the White Knights. However, the bodies were starting to pile up as some shots found their target, slowly forming a sort of protective barrier between them and the mass of White Knights.

"Master!" Fortis shouted. "Do you think it's possible for sabers to break from over use?" Fortis had stolen a saber from one of the White Knights and was now fighting with dual blades as well.

"I'm sure we will find out by the day's end the way this lot is going," replied Biaci.

Meanwhile, Duplex Edge was starting to get angry. "I hate you all," she said angrily, screaming as she stabbed a saber through one's throat. While she withdrew the blade, she parried another incoming strike, fired a bolt at three, and picked up a second blade. Now all three Dark Knights were fighting with dual blades.

"Master, she needs help. They sense she is weaker," Fortis said, sounding concerned, as a shot landed near Duplex Edge.

"Let her be, she is doing fine. Duplex, it's okay. Lose yourself. It was these bastards that put your parents to death; now exact your revenge on them," Biaci ordered, as she knocked a blade back into the owner's chest. Her own saber flew back to her hand and she continued to parry incoming blows.

"Killtooth said rage does no good. Anger is fine; rage will get you killed," Edge replied, sounding out of breath.

"If you don't, you will die; it's time to go mad, for what they have done to us here, our home."

Suddenly a burst of purple light came billowing over their heads and cleared. A circle of dead White Knight's hilts laid around them. For a moment, this stopped the attack as the remaining White Knights fell back to regroup.

Duplex Agens stepped forward, and said, "She is right. Next time, use your rage. Rockwell wasn't with them; we need him."—she turned and waved them back to the barricade—"They won't attack again. They will take half an hour at least."

~

"Admiral Soemu, report. You ready to proceed?" Admiral Takeo asked.

"Soon as the clock strikes zero, we will race you to Rriban" Soemu soundly replied.

"Good,"—Takeo smiled—"I look forward to hearing what the Dragomire jump smoke looked like as we leave you in our trail; Dragomire out."

"You heard him, crew. The honor of the Morgan Rice is at stake. Make sure we are first to jump in two minutes," Soemu ordered.

The time device flashed two minutes.

"I see. We are all prepped and ready to go, Admiral?" Lord Thant asked, taking the Admiral by surprise.

"My Lord, forgive me, however, you know you don't have authorization in this. So why are you here?" the Admiral questioned.

"My place is on the bridge. If you were to be killed, you will need me to take over your ship, right?" replied Thant, as the time flashed one minute thirty seconds.

"I have my ship's Captain for that," Soemu said, and pointed to the Captain.

Lord Thant fired an electrical bolt that killed the Captain instantly. "Thank you for pointing him out to me. Anyone else? I wouldn't make another move; tell your crew to stand down," he ordered.

They had all raised their weapons, pointing at Lord Thant.

"The only one that will be dead is you, and their fire bolts will be reflected back to their owners," Thant remarked to the Admiral.

"Forty seconds remaining," the automated voice stated.

"What do you want?" asked the Admiral.

"Authorization, and I cannot have it until you're dead." With that, Thant's fire saber went through Admiral Soemu's chest, followed by a rain of energy bolts flying everywhere, and just as Thant said, each and every one was reflected back.

"Dragomire to Morgan Rice, see you there out," sounded on the radio as the Dragomire, followed by the rest of the entire fleet, jumped out of the system. The Morgan Rice, with the entire bridge crew dead, stayed exactly where it was. As Lord Thant sat down in the command chair, he sealed the bridge, and set off the ship's carbon monoxide gas to eliminate the ship's crew. He didn't need them to fly the ship; he can say he saved the ship from capture. Tell them the truth, the traitor had sabotaged the ship. However, it was clear Sarah had failed or betrayed him; she would suffer for it.

The Dragomire and the fleet arrived to see the White Knight Super Dreadnaught jump and leave the system.

Soon as it jumped, the remaining parts of the ship's exhaust fell off the ship. As a result, as soon as they had jumped, they arrived in the adjourning sector stuck at normal speed.

~

Back on Rriban, Rockwell had run back inside of the HQ.

"Commander Douglas, you need to leave now, before they blockade the planet and the system. The ship is out back; it will take you out of system. We will hold for as long as we can."

"General, I promise I will return," Commander Douglas replied.

"Commander, I hereby promote you to the rank of General. When you leave, you will be the last of the officer's stationed here, so you deserve the rank. I don't know if Coroscate will confirm it, I cannot say. However, in my eyes, you are a General," he finished, placing General Chester's rank insignia on Douglas' collar, signifying he was now General Douglas.

"Go now," he ordered. With that, General Douglas got into the ship with a Republic pilot. They made it up and out of orbit through the backside of the planet, to avoid being picked up as they left. The ship jumped, ensuring there would be at least one survivor.

~

"Why did you do that? We were holding them off; they were not getting past us," demanded Biaci.

"Exactly, and the moment you launched your trap, they saw what you had planned. They held Rockwell back; we need him. The next attack, we must make sure he leads the charge. No smoke shot next time," Duplex Agens ordered.

"That will give away the only advantage. Are you going to stay with us and fight?" Biaci demanded.

"I will not have to," replied Agens. The sound of her voice was drowned out by the activation of Biaci's fire saber.

"We need you there, Master… If you won't be there, then you could easily slip away from battle and break your promise again." Biaci started to take slow paces forward toward Duplex Agens.

"What is going on, Master? We need to fight them, not each other." Fortis said. Duplex Edge came up beside her and placed a hand on Fortis' right wrist to hold her back.

"A master cannot have two Apprentices. Your master has started the offer of combat," Duplex Edge whispered into Fortis' ear.

"Biaci, I will overlook this and give you a chance to withdraw your challenge. You gave your word," demanded Agens.

"Like you told me you were with my brother's child, just like you used me to kill my own brother. Now you expect us to go out there, just the three of us again, with no smoke barrage? We will be slaughtered. If so, not before I kill you."

Biaci somersaulted towards Duplex Agens, who drew her saber at the last second and reflected Biaci's strike down to the left, then punched her hard in the left cheek. Biaci dropped her saber, and with her free hand, Biaci grabbed the Agens' robes with both hands and kneed her hard with her knee into Agens' stomach winding her making Agens drop her blade.

Going into hand to hand combat, both women ceased to be anything relative to human, transforming into something more like savage beasts.

"Where was this when I first trained you, Apprentice?" asked Agens, just as she grabbed Biaci's fist, blocking her from punching her in the stomach.

"Rriban has hardened me, seeing what they did, knowing what you did to me, to my brother." Agens' fist landed in Biaci's face, cutting the upper right corner of her eye.

Desperate, Biaci grabbed hold of Agens and bit into the flesh around her neck, drawing blood. Agens suddenly stopped her advance, and Biaci took the advantage by pouncing onto Agens, making her collapse to the ground. However, as she landed, Agens lifted her foot just at the right time. As Biaci landed, the kick went straight up into her groin, making Biaci double over in pain.

Both women laid there on their backs, motionless, panting, trying to catch their breath, exhausted. "I am sorry, Biaci. I loved your brother. There was no way I could of killed him. I proved to be the stronger one out of us two, but you are my equal."

At those words said by Agens, Biaci pounced up, sitting astride Agens with a small dagger pointing at her bleeding throat.

Duplex Edge had to restrain Fortis from moving forward. Then they noticed Duplex Agens' small blade sinking into the small of Biaci's back.

"Do you remember, Sis? I warned you of this in your very first lesson. You over extended and you attacked me, not knowing for sure you can win, and now you feel the blade…."

Biaci didn't get to reply, as she was blasted off Duplex Agens and slammed into a wall.

"Enough! The Master and Apprentice fight is not valid here. If you kill, you will be committing murder. You were never announced as my Saber's Apprentice," the Emperor bellowed.

Biaci stared directly at the Emperor with a stern look. "You may not believe me, but ask our young Duplex Edge. You will believe her."

"It's true; I was ordered never to announce you as Duplex's Apprentice,"

Duplex Edge stated.

"So if I have no Master, I'm stuck not able to advance, although having an Apprentice of my own?" Biaci asked.

"Master Biaci, you have earned my respect. You and your Apprentice have saved my Rriban Consequia, led them back into a force the Republic will know forever. They will forever be afraid of our Consequias," the Emperor announced. "Looks like the rest will have to wait, we are about to be alerted."

"The White Knights are approaching!" Captain Jack shouted.

"Fear not, Biaci. I will be joining you this time," the Emperor stated with a cold tone. Everything went silent as Dark Knights Master Biaci, Fortis, Duplex Edge and Duplex Agens walked forward to meet the enemy.

The Emperor placed a hand Agens' shoulder once past the barricade. The Emperor's Saber stopped instantly as the others kept going.

Eight Dark Royal Guards were there; one turned quickly and saluted to Agens. She noticed it was Captain Tyrik.

"Master Sergio, I do believe, unless I am wrong, that is the Emperor coming out to meet our men." he said quite calmly.

"It is, General," Sergio confirmed.

"Then we have no choice, we must advance." He looked to see if there were any objections; none were received.

"Gentleman," he said, shaking their hands. "It was an honor. Forward!!"

No drums this time. As they moved forward the Dark Empire shuttles started to land through-out the planet, landing at all the remote cities.

The two sides clashed in the middle of no-man's land. It became an ocean of dead and those waiting to die, as White Knights were being cut down. What remained of the Republic garrison came charging out around them, heading towards the district.

Duplex Agens, seeing this, took her chance now to put up her hood.

"Report Bellis," she ordered.

"Three have been mod. Met up with team one, heading to the last two now," Bellis replied. While everyone was too busy to notice her, Duplex circumvented the battle to finally head into the Intelligence building in search of what they had originally came for.

Duplex Edge was getting angry once again as she was cutting down left, right, and center, White Knights falling by her side. One Knight came in with a thrust and she sliced his arm off. However, his comrade took advantage of the exposed arm and went to slice off her right arm. However at that exact same moment, a Dark Royal Guard came in with his staff and Duplex Edge saw it go straight through her attacker's skull.

She had no time for words. She summoned her saber and moved onto the next target; the guards had started to clear a path for her.

"Here is your chance, Edge," said a voice from behind a mask. "The Emperor orders you to kill the enemy General Rockwell; do not let the other two know your orders."

Although surprised to see Tyrik was there, she didn't have time to do anything other than kill the next White Knight. However, Tyrik, having took the time to talk to her, didn't see the two Knights coming from behind. They pierced his armor chest plate and he fell to his knees.

"Tell Killtooth…" he started to say, as he stuck out his hand right before the Knight decapitated him.

"Aarrgh!! Nooo!" A burst of energy emanated from Edge as she saw Tyrik being killed. It forced everyone back and she spearheaded straight to the two Knights who had killed Tyrik. By the time she was done, there was nothing left of their masticated bodies.

"Focus the rage…" the Emperor's voice rang inside of her head.

No longer did the White Knights think she was weakest. In fact, they stayed clear, preferring the Emperor over entangling with her, and the Emperor was already certain death.

"Apprentice, Edge, we need to capture him. He is over there," she pointed. Edge had seen Rockwell and stormed towards him, slicing any lingering White Knights along the way.

Bombs and shells flew overhead, inches from her ears, however, they could have been miles away as she was zoned out. This was rage; this was blood lust. She was seeing red. She was almost within reach of Rockwell when Master Ramon sidestepped his way in front of her.

He didn't bother wasting time saluting; he went straight for her face with his Saber. As a response, all she did was tilt her head as she stood there letting him have the strike.

"That's one," she said, as the blade went by her right ear. Ramon attempted to follow the thrust with a side cut to follow the tilting head. However, she just simply ducked under, then leaned back up and stood straight looking at him.

"That's two," she stated. Ramon, not letting Edge frustrate him, attempted another lunge attack to the stomach, which Edge just danced around.

"That's three." With that, she focused on his throat and began to suck the air from his lungs. Blood started boiling up into his throat, draining down his windpipe. Ramon attempted to scream, but it was impossible. He was drowning on his own boiling blood, and he crashed to her feet dead.

"You're out," she said, smiling.

She carried on her pacing, ignoring all those around her. Except Fortis suddenly cried out for help. Edge turned to see she was pinned down and had lost one of her sabers.

Duplex Edge walked up to her at the same time Biaci did. Edge simply grabbed hold of the backs of the two that were pinning Fortis and threw them using the Dark Power. They crashed into the building and their bodies fell to the floor like rag dolls.

"You okay?" she asked as she offered a hand down to Fortis.

"Look out!" Edge turned on the spot to see Master Sergio poised behind her, about to strike. She was done for, except Biaci used the Power to blast Sergio towards the Emperor, who caught him in his right hand and snapped his neck like a twig.

Biaci had gotten to Rockwell first. "You are our prisoner, sir."

"I thought the order was no prisoners?" Rockwell questioned as he dropped his weapon to the ground.

At that time, one of the container ships landed in the district. Upon opening, it was completely empty, no military force whatsoever.

"General, order your men to surrender," the Emperor's voice sounded in his mind.

"WHITE KNIGHTS, DROP your arms. Republic forces, it's over. As the commanding officer of the Republic forces, I hereby surrender to you." "Dark Knight Edge, escort General Rockwell to the back," ordered Biaci.

"Master Biaci, you are hereby my Saber from this point forth. Go with Duplex Edge," the Emperor ordered.

Fortis, Edge, and Biaci marched Rockwell away in cuffs. More ships landed around the Emperor.

Duplex Edge got to the room Biaci told her to take Rockwell to, the same one where they held his son.

"General," she said handing a small object to him. He didn't even bother to look at it while he held it in his hand.

"Go on, get it over with," he retorted. Then at that exact same time, multiple things happened all at once. Duplex Edge stabbed Rockwell through the heart of with her saber.

Just as Biaci came into the room, seeing this, she struck out at Edge, killing her as she had attempted to stop Edge's attack. However, with Edge moving forward, it sliced into her chest instead of deflecting the blade.

"What have you done?!" shouted Biaci, as Fortis came running to see the mess. The Carbon Medallion of the Emperor's Saber laid at Rockwell's feet.

"Fortis, do you know who their next in command is?" she shouted. She cradled Edge in her arms; her own sister laid dying in her arms because of her Master.

At the same time, Duplex approached slowly from behind to stand alongside the Emperor.

"You have it? …is he?" asked the Emperor.

The Emperor's Saber did not say a word. She held one datapad below her arm, and one single tear dropped from her left eye.

"Needed to be punished, he did," the Emperor said slowly, placing a hand on her shoulder. "Your time as my Saber is at an end Duplex Agens…"

"But…!" she turned to protest. He raised his hand to silence her.

"This will be the third time. I cannot allow you to avoid it anymore. No one is wanting to replace them in fear you will kill them. So you need to become one. Biaci, who is unknown, will be your replacement."

The wrist communicator vibrated on Agens wrist with the sound of Bellis' voice, "Task complete, my Lord."

"Acknowledged. Return," Duplex Agens said.

"Be happy, my child. You've helped secure. This will go on forever and the hate will continue, and you exacted your revenge."

~

Aboard the Dragomire Bridge, it was just Lord Thant present with the ship's crew lying dead at his feet.

He had with him the terminal device he had opened waiting to receive any kind of message. He also had the picture of Fidus with him.

He had been waiting for hours; no news came from the battle, from either Dark Imperial or Rockwell. Although he felt certain of the outcome, he felt happy that he knew at the end, he would become Emperor. With them on the planet, they would never expect what hit them on Rriban or at Kaas City at the same time. He would arrive back to take control of the Empire.

The terminal flashed, "Commanding officer Rockwell, life signature terminated; Rockwell KIA."

So there it was, Rockwell had been killed. Now he was the next senior ranking Republic officer here. Lord Thant, leading member of the Dark Council, soon to be the next Emperor, is now also the leading Republic officer.

He started to laugh at how easily simple it was to trick and manipulate everyone. He started to type the code Rockwell had given him earlier.

"Your Master never figured out, and will never figure out, who it was that killed her mommy now." He finished the last of the forty two number combination, followed by his voice authorization and hit transmit.

"There, it is done. Now, he was the Emperor." Again, he started laughing a mechanical laugh, just as the picture of Fidus started peeping.

"What?!" He exclaimed, as he smashed the thick wooden frame around the picture. Several things dropped out: Cryptic M's bloody name tag of Cryptic M, a picture of Duplex Agens holding the Carbon Medallion of the Emperor's Saber, showing the clip of a ping pierced through the medallion. As he flipped the picture, he saw one more name tag, Reader's Eight name tag, which Duplex Edge had placed on the statue, which was now presently peeping.

Written on the back, "I believe these belong to you. I know it was you. Signed E.S."

Lord Thant laughed and laughed and laughed, until the blast from the Reader Eight badge, laced and made with high volatile explosive, ripped through the entire ship of the Morgan Rice as the ship exploded, leaving only particle dust, only the sound waves of Lord Thant's manic laughing, forever wandering through space.

# 1 MONTH LATER

The Republic drop ship with General Douglas jumped into the system. The Republic 21$^{st}$, 34$^{th}$, and a detachment of White Knights were on board, expecting a fight on their hands as they entered.

The planet from space had changed; the red planet looked like a darker red or dirty orange kind of color.

"Report! " General Douglas said.

"The explosives went off, however, something went wrong. Instead of blowing up the cities and destabilizing the planet's core, they fired the chemicals up into the atmosphere. There is no life at all on the planet anymore. No wild life, nothing. Even the dirt is dead," the ship's Captain said.

"General, scanners are picking up something." Flipping the switch to turn on the view port, they saw a huge floating time device circling the planet in stationary orbit. "What is that on the end?" said the Captain.

"The Gold Medallion of the Emperor, promising to kill us. How long is that any way?" The number on the clock was so high, he knew it was years, just not certain on how long.

"General, the computer says that it will be one hundred and fifty years," the Captain announced. "Sir, so you are saying the Emperor is saying we will die after a hundred and fifty years?"

"We will already be dead; he is talking about the Republic," replied Douglas.

Just then the radio man shouted, "Sir, picking up communications, unknown source."

"Open the channel," ordered Douglas.

"Ha –hah-haaaahahaaa wahwaaahaaa." The sound of Lord Thant's manic laughing came over the radio. Douglas walked over and shut off the signal.

"You were listening to a ghost; they have played their hand well."

~

"My Emperor, forgive me, I still don't understand it all. Why did we have to sacrifice the planet?" Lord Duplex Agens of the Dark Council asked.

"It is simple. Our people wanted revenge for the Rriban defeat. Once we had recovered the planet, they would of wanted peace. Now, they have hatred, and that hate will escape time; our children's children will carry on the hate for what the Republic did to our home planet. We've liberated Rriban; the planet is full of Dark Power energy now, and it will heal when we are done rebuilding. As you know, fear is power. They know we are here; they know the Dark Knights are alive. They have no idea where, when we will strike. However, what I do know, is the planet will be ready to receive the future Dark Knights and they will be ready to carry on the fight because of the hate we gave birth to here," explained the Emperor, as they both walked through the throne room.

"So you've created what seems like peace to the Republic, however, that very peace is the lie, for they know we intend to come," replied Agens.

"As long as there are those who are willing to use their emotions, including anger and hate, not just the happy feeling emotions, as tools, the Dark Knights will live and thrive forever. Passion will beat our enemies. Denying your own emotions will only serve to help the enemy win, so get angry, get passionate, and destroy all those that oppose you from whatever you wish to achieve."

*The End*

Christopher Blythe Bartram / ISBN-13: 9780692581230

## AUTHOR'S NOTES

Although the sinking of the A.H.S Centaur was very tragic, we must be careful of jumping to a decision based on what we read by one source alone. Any loss of life is sad, however, it was during a time of war. The Japanese, we discovered, were willing to commit suicide rather than surrender to the American forces. Japan did not ratify the Geneva Convention into law, so therefore, cannot be held to the same standards. Japanese tactics were seen as desperate and brutal, whereas the Japanese of the time would view their tactics as unweaving loyalty.

The Captain of the Japanese submarine, believed what his officers told him about hearing how America is putting Japanese into camps. Believing the rumors, their wounded were being slaughtered by the Allies. Perhaps he saw something that we don't know, and would not be in the Australian reports. There is also a reason why the Tribunal didn't find any evidence.

Because it was an Australian ship is the reason everyone was up in arms with the Allies, with perfect ammunition for their propaganda machine. It was war, and with it, the truth dies, so how can we trust what is written by the Australians? Do you really believe the report was not prejudice in favor of playing Australia as a victim? So we may never know what truly happened. Only those who witnessed it firsthand will know.

Just keep in mind and be observant the victim(s) will always be louder. South Korea may say such things as North Korea is preparing for Nuclear war, when in fact all they did is a test or move outdated equipment. South Korea has a reason to be scared; it is right on their door step. Whereas in the United States, the perspective of what North Korea may be doing is somewhat more clear. Or in more recent events, France didn't want to do anything in regards to supporting the anti-terror efforts and left it to America, Iraq, and Syria to fight ISIS alone. Then as soon as they got attacked, it suddenly became an act of war and brought Europe shaking in its boots. Perhaps it was a red flag operation to produce the reaction needed to get the European countries to do more against ISIS. I'm not saying it was or wasn't; you, the reader, I want to make sure you open your eyes to what the world is like and don't be fooled into thinking North Korea is the only country guilty of brain washing its own people. Governments of all countries and nations will use any event, good, bad or as tragic as the sinking of the A.H.S Centaur, to promote what is in their best interest.

So make sure no one tells you anything. Make up your own mind.

## A.H.S CENTAUR (HOSPITAL SHIP)

The *Centaur*, 2/3rd Australian Hospital Ship, was a motor passenger ship converted in early 1943 for use as a hospital ship. In November 1941 it had rescued survivors of the German auxiliary cruiser *Kormoran* after it had sunk and been sunk by HMAS *Sydney*.

On 12 May 1943 the *Centaur* sailed unescorted from Sydney at 0945 hours carrying her crew and normal staff, as well as stores and equipment of the 2/12th Field Ambulance but no patients. It was sunk without warning by a torpedo from a Japanese submarine on 14 May 1943 at approximately 0400 hours, its position being approximately 27°17' S, 153°58' E about 50 miles east north-east of Brisbane.

Of the 332 persons on board, only 64 survived. These survivors spent 35 hours on rafts before being rescued. Sister Ellen Savage, the only one of twelve nursing sisters on board to survive, though injured herself, gave great help to the other survivors and was awarded the George Medal for this work.

The ship had been appropriately lit and marked to indicate that it was a hospital ship and its sinking was regarded as an atrocity. The Australian Government delivered an official protest to Japan over the incident. The Japanese did not acknowledge responsibility for the incident for many years and the War Crimes Tribunal could not identify the responsible submarine. However, the Japanese official war history makes clear that it was submarine 1-177, under the command of Lt Commander Nakagawa who had sunk the *Centaur*. Lt Commander Nakagawa was convicted as a war criminal for firing on survivors of the *British Chivalry* which his ship had sunk in the Indian Ocean.

List of the crew of A.H.S Centaur
https://www.awm.gov.au/sites/default/files/encyclopedia/centaur/AWM54_409_9_1.pdf

source: https://www.awm.gov.au/encyclopedia/centaur/

Christopher Blythe Bartram / ISBN-13: 9780692581230